Edwin Hodder

The Seventh Earl of Shaftesbury, K. G., As Social Reformer

Edwin Hodder

The Seventh Earl of Shaftesbury, K. G., As Social Reformer

ISBN/EAN: 9783337295592

Printed in Europe, USA, Canada, Australia, Japan

Cover: Foto ©Raphael Reischuk / pixelio.de

More available books at **www.hansebooks.com**

THE SEVENTH
EARL OF SHAFTESBURY,
K.G.,

as Social Reformer.

BY

EDWIN HODDER,

*Author of " The Life and Work of the Seventh Earl of Shaftesbury, K.G." ; " The Life of Samuel Morley " ; " John MacGregor (Rob Roy)," " George Smith, of Coalville,"
etc., tc.*

LONDON:

JAMES NISBET & CO., LIMITED,

21, BERNERS STREET.

1897.

PREFACE.

I T was my high honour to be chosen by the "good" Earl of Shaftesbury to be his biographer, and, in 1886, it was my privilege to give to the world the full story of his life—political, social, domestic, philanthropic, and religious. It was, of necessity, a lengthy narrative, occupying three bulky volumes and sixteen hundred pages of print.

The present work is confined to one aspect of his career—that of Social Reformer—and is intended to set before the reader in a brief form a *résumé* of those important movements to which he devoted his life, standing out pre-eminently as the champion of the defenceless and oppressed, and winning for himself a name that will live for ever in the annals of this country as the Friend of the Working Man, and *the* great Social Reformer of the nineteenth century.

EDWIN HODDER.

HEATHERDENE, HAREWOOD ROAD,
SOUTH CROYDON.

CONTENTS.

THE SEVENTH

EARL OF SHAFTESBURY, K.G.

CHAPTER I.

EARLY CAREER.

ANTONY ASHLEY COOPER, seventh Earl of
Shaftesbury, was born in Grosvenor Square
on April 28th, 1801.   His father was for many years
Chairman of Committees in the House of Lords.
His mother was a daughter of the fourth Duke of
Marlborough.   The ancestors of the Earl, both on
his mother's and his father's side, were distinguished
men.   The first Earl of Shaftesbury was the famous
minister of Charles II. ; the third Earl was the
equally famous author of the "Characteristics";
the second, fourth, and fifth Earls achieved no distinction or left no mark on the history of their
times.   The sixth Earl, Cropley Ashley, succeeded
to the title on the death of his brother in 1811.

The first qualification for the work before him of
the great Englishman, Christian philanthropist, and

I

social reformer, whose life we are now to consider, was his birthright of rank and position. He was always sensible of the vantage ground thus afforded him, and it may be well to ask, in passing, whether it is easy to overestimate the gain to the whole community, that not every citizen should be forced to spend his prime in climbing high enough above his fellows to be able to render them effectual service?

He had other congenital personal gifts—manly good looks and a striking presence, which, it cannot be gainsaid, help a man more than we sometimes think, and which certainly helped him when he endeavoured to inspire his humble fellow-countrymen with his noble and elevated character. Gifts of intellect were added, such as has been truly said might well have inclined him to take a part in the higher walks of political life. Immense energy, untiring industry, indomitable perseverance, and the noble ambition which covets, not personal distinction for its own sake, but that honour which in its highest form is to have " the answer of a good conscience " ; a command over language which clothed his thoughts, written or spoken, in right and forcible words ; an unrivalled memory ; a keen power of observation ; a statesmanlike faculty in choosing his instruments ; an insight into character, and a depth of sympathy, developed by special circumstances, which was the human motive of his strenuous labours, together with a vivid imagination and a heart which craved for love and approval, were the natural equipment of the knightly soul destined to engage in more single combats on behalf of the weak and defenceless than any paladin of the Middle Ages.

A further qualification for his life-work was the sorrow and sadness and pitiful loneliness of his childhood and early surroundings. His father, an excellent chairman of committees—a duty he discharged faithfully for forty years—was engrossed in the cares of public life, and had acquired harsh and dictatorial habits, which may have facilitated the business of the House of Lords, but certainly did not add to the charm of private intercourse. He brought up his son with great severity, moral and physical, in respect both of mind and body, his opinion being that to render a child obedient it should be in a constant fear of its father and mother. Throughout his life he had no sympathy with his son, and for long periods was totally estranged from him. Nor did the heart of the child find any resting-place in the love of its mother: she was wholly absorbed in the daily round of fashionable pleasures, and found neither time nor inclination to give attention to the proper duties of motherhood.

Happily, however, there was one who really cared for and loved the child. This was one Maria Millis, the housekeeper, to whose care he was confided: it was she who taught him his first prayer—a prayer that until the day of his death he constantly used; it was she who, from the lessons of Holy Scripture, led him to desire to "be good and to do good"; it was she who was his spiritual mother, his only sympathetic friend, his "special providence"; and to her influence he traced very much, perhaps all, of the inspiration of his later life. She left him a handsome gold watch, and throughout his life he never wore any other. " He was fond, even to the last, of showing it, and would say, 'That was given me by the best friend I ever had in the world.' " *

When he was about seven years old Maria Millis died, and the child was left to the tender mercies of servants, who seemed to be lacking in the common instincts of humanity ; for, strange and almost incredible as it may appear, if we had not the facts from Lord Shaftesbury himself, he was often kept for days without sufficient food, until he was pinched with starvation ; he knew what it was to lie awake many weary nights in winter, all through the long

---

* The following anecdote is taken from a Report of the Ashley Mission, Bethnal Green, founded by the Hon. William Ashley, Lord Shaftesbury's younger brother :—

"'The watch which Maria Millis bequeathed to him when he was seven years old, some half-century later, on the occasion of one of his visits to a disreputable neighbourhood, was stolen from its owner. Lord Shaftesbury immediately advertised his loss and his great value for the missing property. 'There is honour among thieves.' Soon after, a cab drew up to his door in Grosvenor Square ; a tremendous ring was given, a large canvas bag was deposited on the threshold, and the two men who brought it were promptly driven off. The bag was opened. It was found not only to contain the precious watch, but the young culprit who had known no better than to steal it, together with a written request that he might meet with his deserts. It need scarcely be said that the restoration of Maria Millis's legacy was rewarded with his pardon, while a fresh start in life was afforded him, by the good education of the Reformatory School to which he was forthwith sent."

hours suffering from cold ; he was the victim of many cruel and petty tyrannies, and spent the years of his young life, that should have been only bright and joyous, in a state of utter misery, without a friend in the world to cheer him with sympathy and loving-kindness.

On entering his eighth year the lad was sent to a school, which has latterly given place to a lunatic asylum—Manor House, Chiswick. It was a fashionable and successful school, kept by Dr. Thomas Horne, a good classical scholar, the father of Sir William Horne, Attorney-General under Earl Grey, and afterwards Master in Chancery. It is a truism that there are as wide differences in the mental as in the physical constitution of boys. Lord Lyndhurst, who went to this same school under the same master, gives a somewhat glowing account of it, altogether different from that of Lord Shaftesbury, who, late in life, said, " The memory of that place makes me shudder ; it is repulsive to me even now. I think there never was such a wicked school before or since. The place was bad, wicked, filthy ; and the treatment was starvation and cruelty." There is, perhaps, a little exaggeration in this description, the result of an overwrought and sensitive nature ; but the fact remains that to him, whatever it might have been to any one else, life at that school was a prolonged torture.

It is not necessary to dwell upon this period of his life, but some knowledge of these painful experiences is necessary to the true appreciation of his subsequent career. " No one who knew Lord Shaftesbury could fail to observe in him an air of melancholy, a certain sombreness and sadness, which habitually surrounded him like an atmosphere. It was no doubt to be attributed, in great measure, to the scenes of suffering and sorrow which were continually before him ; but it was also largely due to the fact that there had been no light-heartedness in his childhood, and that the days to which most men look back with the keenest delight were only recalled by him with a shrinking sense of horror. But it is important to the understanding of his life in another aspect [that of a social reformer] that this record of his unhappy childhood should be given. Those early years of sorrow were the years in which he was graduating for his great life-work. He had suffered oppression ; henceforth his life would be devoted to fighting the battles of the oppressed. He had known loneliness, and cold, and hunger ; henceforth he would plead the cause of the poor, the lonely, the suffering, and the hungry. He had known the loss of a happy childhood ; henceforth he would labour, as long as life should last, to bring joy and gladness to the hearts and homes of little children." *

In 1811 the father, succeeding to the title, went to live at St. Giles, the family seat in Dorsetshire ; and in 1813, after five years at the Manor House School, Chiswick, the son was sent, at about twelve years old, to Harrow, and was placed under the

* "The Life and Work of the Seventh Earl of Shaftesbury, K.G.," by Edwin Hodder (Cassell & Co., Ltd. 1886. In three volumes), vol. i., p. 42.

care and in the house of the Head Master, Dr. Butler. Here a happier era dawned upon him; he found friends whom he could love and esteem—among them the loving, large-hearted Sir Harry Verney, afterwards distinguished as a philanthropist not less than in other important respects.

It was while he was at Harrow that an incident occurred which gave shape and tone to his character, and became the starting-point in his life of philanthropic labour. Walking alone one day down Harrow Hill he encountered a drunken group shouting out Bacchanalian songs as they staggered along with a coffin containing the remains of a deceased comrade. Presently, turning a corner, they let their burden drop, and broke out into foul and horrible language. Struck with unspeakable horror at the ghastly scene, the lad, after gazing at it for a few moments as if spellbound, exclaimed, "Good heavens! can this be permitted simply because the man was poor and friendless?" And then and there he registered a vow that, with God's help, he would thenceforth make the cause of the poor his own. And faithfully he kept that vow.*

Soon after he attained his fifteenth year young Lord Ashley, for so we must call him till his accession to the Earldom in his fifty-first year, left Harrow,—

* A suggestion was made in the "Life and Work of Lord Shaftesbury," vol. i., p. 49, that a suitable monument should mark the spot where this resolution was made, eventuating in the freedom of thousands of the poor and helpless. We are delighted to hear that a movement is now on foot (1897) to carry out this suggestion.

where he had obtained prizes and reached the sixth form,—and went to reside with a clergyman in Derbyshire. Here, if he did not, as he tells us, learn much, he at least acquired a taste for the innocent pleasures of a rustic life. In 1819, after two years with his private tutor in Derbyshire, his father decided on his going up to Christ Church, Oxford, where he soon began to take life in greater earnest, and made up for what he considered " much wasted time" by such exemplary assiduity in his studies that in three years' time, to his own intense surprise, he came out of the schools a first-class man in classics in 1822.

To somewhere about this period we may assign an amusing anecdote, "told by one who was present, whose word is above doubt, and who still lives. We tell it * in the words of the witness : 'At Edinburgh, where I was visiting my sister, I first made acquaintance with the young Lord Ashley, who was the handsomest young man I ever saw, full of fun and frolic, very tall, and his countenance radiant with youthful hope. He had come down to Scotland with his cousin, George Howard, afterwards Lord Morpeth, whom he was very anxious to make as intimate with his friends as he already was himself; but Mr. Howard, besides being naturally shy, was quite a stranger, and did not see the pleasure or advantage of the introduction. However, it was effected. We heard a scuffle outside the drawing-room door, which was suddenly thrown open, and he rushed head foremost into the middle of the

* *Church Times*, December 17th, 1886.

room, projected as from a battering ram, while Lord Ashley shouted, " Enter the Honourable George Howard ! "　Of course there was an end of all shyness after this.' "

This will seem strange to those who remember the habitual and unbroken gravity of the Puritan Earl in later years, but there is abundance of evidence to show that the "unbroken gravity" was very gradually acquired ; for he acknowledges in his diaries the enjoyment of "a round of laughing and pleasure," and even speaks of "loving joviality"; while every member of his family testifies that to the end of his life he relished a joke and possessed a fund of quiet, subtle humour.　His old friend Sir George Burns, with whom Lord Shaftesbury was very intimate, has testified that, when he was on his annual visit to Wemyss Bay, "it was proverbial that wherever the ripple of laughter was to be heard and the most fun was going on, there Lord Shaftesbury was invariably to be found." *

After leaving Oxford he travelled for some time, according to custom ; and in his twenty-sixth year, at the General Election of 1826, he entered Parliament, after a severe contest, as member for Woodstock, then the pocket borough of the House of Marlborough. At that time his future had not, even in his own thoughts, assumed definite shape ; his religion was the paramount influence over his conduct, and he was habitually looking for Divine help and guidance to keep his conscience unsullied and to make straight

* "Sir George Burns, Bart.: His Times and Friends," p. 405.

his paths before him.   He had resolved generally to plead the cause of the poor and friendless, but he had not yet found the opportunity which he sought. For purely political life he felt himself to be unfitted. He was too sensitive, too diffident, to make a successful leader ; he distrusted himself and underrated his own abilities ; he possessed a constitutional shyness which made it a pleasure to him to pass unnoticed ; and he had fallen into a habit, which he never could quite shake off, of analysing his own motives, principles, and actions, in a morbid fashion, constantly cherishing self-depreciation and fears of failure, though he longed to do good work for his country.

About this time a friendship, only interrupted by death, sprang up between the Duke of Wellington and young Lord Ashley.   His enthusiasm for the great Duke was unbounded, and it was only increased by his prolonged intimacy.

When Lord Ashley entered Parliament, as a Tory, Lord Liverpool, the Premier, was fast approaching the close of his long official career, and in the following year (1827) Canning became Prime Minister in his stead.   Ashley was offered a post in the Government, the negotiations being opened by his great friend Mrs. (afterwards Lady) Canning ; but out of loyalty to the Duke he refused the offer. " With me," he said, " the Duke is the chief consideration."

Four months later Canning died, and in the January following Lord Ashley took office under the Duke of Wellington, for whose sake he had before refused it. He was appointed to be a Commissioner of the India Board of Control, and held that office—almost the only office of profit he ever held—till Lord Grey's accession to power in 1830. This situation afforded him not only a golden opportunity for displaying his inherent ability, but became a source of great satisfaction to him in after life. During the Mutiny era in 1857 he could look back with pleasure to the part he had taken on the Suttee question—that is, the practice of burning widows at the death of their husbands. It was predicted that a revolt would follow, but his opinion that it would be safe was justified by the event. "The whole of India," he said, "was satisfied that it was right, when Lord William Bentinck appealed to those great principles of the human heart which are implanted by the hand of God. . . . If you appeal to the conscience, depend upon it the millions will go along with you."

During his tenure of office the establishment of " Scientific Corporations for the Institution and Improvement of Horticulture and Husbandry throughout the Provinces of India " was one of his schemes for the benefit of our great dependency, the moral results of the community of pursuits to be thus induced between the European and the native, being one main consideration to be kept in view. The salt monopoly deeply interested him as one affecting most nearly the comforts of several millions ; and the course he took in middle life with regard to the opium question, and in advanced age with respect to the progress of the factory system in India and its accompanying cruelties, when unrestricted, inspire the wish that the India Board could longer have retained such services.

Lord Ashley's first speech in Parliament was delivered in February 1828, in support of a Bill to Amend the Law for the Regulation of Lunatic Asylums, and it sounded the key-note of his Parliamentary career, although it was not until 1833 that he was to send forth the clarion sounds that were to stir the nation.

In June 1830 he married Lady Emily Cowper, daughter of the future Lady Palmerston—" a wife," to use his own language, fondly written in the evening of his life, " as good, as true, and as deeply beloved as God ever gave to man."

Shortly before this happy event Lord Ashley had been returned, at the General Election, to represent Dorchester; but he only held the seat a year, the rejection of the Reform Bill in 1831 having brought about another dissolution of Parliament. On account of his popularity and local influence he was then chosen to contest the county of Dorset in the anti-reform interest. His opponent was the Hon. William Ponsonby (afterwards Lord de Mauley), and the fight was long and severe, lasting for fifteen days; but Lord Ashley won the contest, the expense of it exceeding £15,000—an amount which, notwithstanding the promises of his political friends, he had to pay almost entirely alone; and being then, and ever after, a comparatively poor man, he became involved in very harassing financial difficulties. For the next fifteen years he continued to represent the county in Parliament.

It will be well in this place to define, as well as we can, Lord Ashley's attitude towards the Reform Bill of 1832, and to politics generally. On the jubilee of the passing of the Reform Bill (1882) the question was asked in the *Times* whether any of the survivors of the Reform Parliament would hold to the opinion then expressed, " that the sun of England had set for ever." Lord Shaftesbury replied :—

" I am one of the survivors, but I do not recollect that I ever expressed that opinion, nor was it the opinion of the great statesmen who at that time resisted the measure. They maintained that it would lead eventually to large and organic changes ; that it would overthrow the Established Church, and destroy the independence of the House of Lords, if it did not altogether annihilate its existence.

" They never contemplated these issues as immediate ; they generally believed that about thirty years would elapse before the full and permanent effects were visible. In this they were right. The Household Suffrage Act of 1867, followed by the introduction of the Ballot, gave the final stamp to the future character of legislation. One enactment yet remains —the enactment of Household Suffrage for the counties. This measure will affect the tenure and transmission of property in every form, as the other measures have affected the principle and action of political institutions."

It is somewhat difficult to define Lord Shaftesbury's

exact place as a politician. Shortly after he entered
Parliament, as Lord Ashley, we find him in doubt
between a career of party and personal ambition,
and complete retirement from public life. His ambition was at that time as keen as his despondency
with regard to his own abilities was morbid ; but
such was the state of the times that he saw no alternative between taking part in the endless round of
intrigue for place and power, without any worthy or
ultimate object, and studies or moral solitude, there
being apparently no obvious connection between
politics and, in a large sense, the good of mankind.
The idea of such a connection would in all probability have been scouted as a Utopian, if not a
dangerous dream.

The political principles upon which he started in
life were, however, fixed, and he never deviated
from them. He was so little a partisan that both
sides have been anxious, at certain periods, to claim
him as their own ; but he never wavered by a hair's
breadth from the three articles of his political creed—
the Crown, the hereditary Peerage, and the Established Church, institutions on the maintenance of
which he considered the happiness of the country to
depend. He opposed the Reform Bill of 1832, as we
have seen ; he led the opposition in the House of
Lords to the Reform Bill of 1867 and to the Ballot
Act of 1872, and he always used the word " demo-
cracy " as a term of reproach.

The fact is now generally recognised that the
history of this country has passed in recent years

from a political to a social stage. The questions that
most interest us now are questions of social, and not
merely political, importance; and no one man ever
did more to effect the change that has come over our
notion of what is important than the subject of this
memoir. Whether he was always right in his opinion
of how the popular welfare was to be promoted;
whether he did not attribute too much importance to
the action of the State; whether in the ardour of his
philanthropy he would not, unless restrained by more
worldly persons with cooler heads, have injured what
he wished to benefit, are questions which have given
rise to discussions in the press, but need not be
dealt with here. He might not have been a statesman;
he certainly was not, in the ordinary sense of the
word, a pronounced politician, though he lived amid
the dust of political controversy for more than sixty
years, and always took the keenest interest in politics;
he probably delivered more speeches in both Houses
of the Legislature than any member of either during
the present century who has not been charged with
the responsibility of office. Always retaining Con-
servative principles, he held opinions which had a
flavour of advanced Liberalism; and, as life went on,
he had a distrust of both the great parties in the
State. "To his latest day he held in aversion the
economic doctrines of what is commonly known as
the Manchester School, and in the early part of his
Parliamentary career he broke many a controversial
lance with their greatest champions."

Determined to devote himself to that soundest and

best of political objects, the social elevation of the masses, it was not unnatural that he should, although by no means a man of one idea, measure public men according as they did or did not support the measures in which he was most interested. Judged by this standard, neither Sir Robert Peel nor John Bright, neither Richard Cobden nor Mr. Gladstone, won his admiration or was eulogised by him in his private writings; whereas Macaulay, who was a convert to the Ten Hours Bill, was, on his death, the subject of a just and striking eulogy, which we quote as illustrating the attitude of Lord Shaftesbury's mind in his estimate of men : " His sentiments and expressions were always generous; he never thought that brilliant exploits compensated for the want of moral worth, and he would call a man a villain, a rogue, or an oppressor, whether he were arrayed like Solomon, or in tatters like Lazarus. . . . May I never forget his true and noble speech, made at my request in the House of Commons, on behalf of the factory children ! "

The almost universal testimony is, that there never was an English politician, living or dead, who was so uniformly upright in his public life as Lord Shaftesbury; he had one single aim—to do, at whatever personal sacrifice, what he believed to be best for the country at large; and that on the whole his judgment on politics was exceedingly accurate and far-sighted. Certainly no minister could ever influence him by any paltry or indirect consideration; and again and again he astonished his worldly and more easy-going political allies, or opponents, by disregarding every bait that should tend to divert his footsteps for a moment from the plain path he had set himself to follow.

It is now time to consider in detail what he wrought, and in doing so we must always bear in mind that he was a deeply religious man, "rooted and grounded and settled." From childhood he had a simple but overmastering faith in the omniscience and omnipresence of an over-ruling Providence. God was as real to him as a personal friend; he was always as conscious of His presence as though He were actually standing by his side. This was the source of all his strength, the impetus to all his actions, the deepest of all his convictions; and no one can understand either his character or his motives who does not know the open secret that every plan, every speech, every labour was laid upon the altar as "an offering unto the Lord."

Let one illustration of this phase of his character suffice.

Lord Ashley had been sent to Parliament to defend the Corn Laws; but in 1846, in presence of the Irish famine, that defence was no longer possible. He felt also that good faith to his constituents compelled the resignation of his seat in Parliament, notwithstanding the fact that it would cause him to abandon his Ten Hours Bill and extinguish the projects for which he had laboured incessantly for years. Lady Ashley supported his high-minded resolution, and he wrote in his diary :—

"*Jan.* 15*th.*—Ought I not to be deeply thankful to Almighty God that He has given me a wife capable of every generous self-denial, and prepared to rejoice in it, if it be for the advancement of religion and the welfare of man?"

"*Jan.* 27*th.*—Public necessity and public welfare both demand the repeal of the Corn Laws. I could justify such a vote before God, because I am convinced that it would be for the best for every material and moral interest; but I have entered into relations with men, and I must observe them, though it be to my own detriment. The slight influence I possess is founded on an estimation of character. . . . Far better that I should suffer any loss than give occasion to the enemies of God to blaspheme and say that, 'After all, your religious men, when they come to be tried, are no better than any one else.' Many would say this; many more would think it; and . . . when I have endeavoured and prayed that all my conduct might be to the honour of God, I should have done more in a single hour to cast a stain on 'pious statesmen' than I could render of service to His holy Name in the labours of twenty years.

" I remember, therefore, those blessed texts: 'Seek ye first the kingdom of God and His righteousness, and all these things shall be added unto you'; 'Commit thy way unto the Lord, and He will direct thy paths.' In this hope I will surrender all, and maintain my integrity while I lose my office.

" I shall resign my seat and throw up all my beloved projects; all for which I have sacrificed everything that a public man values ; all that I have begun and all that I have designed. . . . But God's will be done. 'Though He slay me,' said Job, 'yet will I trust in Him.'"

Thus, two days after having re-introduced his Ten Hours Bill into the House of Commons—this time with every prospect of success—he resigned his seat and gave up all for conscience' sake.

CHAPTER II.

TOWARDS the end of the last century, owing principally to the development of machinery and the application of steam power, an enormous extension had been given to the cotton manufactures of England. The great centres where they were carried on became studded with vast mills, surrounded by a densely crowded population ; and a demand for the labour of women and children had been created, which gave rise to frightful abuses and cruelties. A traffic, as revolting as the slave traffic of Africa, had sprung up ; gangs of child-jobbers scoured the country to entrap or purchase thousands of little children of either sex, from five years old and upwards, to sell them into the bondage of factory slaves. The misery and waste of life were terrible, and almost incomprehensible to the present generation. Day and night the iron wheels of the unresting machinery droned and burred with maddening iteration ; and amidst the unceasing din, in an atmosphere polluted by stench and thick with the choking "flew" of the cotton, myriads of these tender little victims were forced to labour, under the lash of brutal overlookers, till nature gave way, or death brought a merciful release.

Any one who studies the question of the deep misery of the English poor, which commenced after the Peace of Paris, increased to an alarming degree after the Reform Act, and attained its maximum during the first years of the present reign, will find ample confirmation in general literature, in the pages of fiction, in poetry, and above all in the cold and hard statistics of Blue Books, as to the state of women and children who worked in factories and in mines, and whose condition was so appalling that it cried aloud for legislation.

Several attempts were made in the early part of the century to alleviate these horrors by legislative enactment ; but the influence of the great mill owners, and the jealousy of political economists, prevented any effectual remedy being applied.

The first Sir Robert Peel, himself a manufacturer, carried, in 1802, a measure to provide for the care and education of the hapless children who were "apprenticed" to manufacturers. The Act had an influence in gradually doing away with the apprentice system, but only indirectly. The manufacturers replaced the apprentices sent from a distance by others who dwelt in the same neighbourhood, and thus relief was only given to one set of children at the expense of another set. This circumstance did not escape the vigilance of Sir Robert, who, in 1819, obtained the assent of Parliament to another measure, which forbade the employment in a cotton factory of any child under nine years of age, or any young person under sixteen for more than twelve hours a day. This Bill, however, only applied to *cotton* factories ; in all other industries infant labour was unregulated. Children of the tenderest age were generally worked for fifteen hours a day with brief intervals for rest and food. Large numbers of them actually perished, worn out by toil, before they attained their full age ; stunted and deformed, the survivors bore on their persons indelible marks of the cruel severity of their labours.

It was not until 1830 that the great and comprehensive movement, with which later on Lord Ashley was to be pre-eminently identified, commenced. This was no less than beneficent legislation for, not children in cotton factories only, but for children employed in the manufacture of textile fabrics throughout the kingdom.

At the end of the session of 1831 Mr. Michael Thomas Sadler, a Tory, an uncompromising opponent of political and religious freedom, but in social matters a humane and earnest philanthropist, and a warm advocate of the interests of the working classes, introduced his famous Ten Hours Bill, the object of which was to restrict the labour both of women and children in the cotton mills to ten hours daily. He succeeded in getting the Bill referred to a Select Committee, but farther progress was barred by the Reform Bill of the following year. At the ensuing General Election, Newark, the borough which he repre-

sented, was disfranchised. He failed to obtain a seat
either for Leeds or Huddersfield, and Robert Southey
specially laments him among the good men thrown
out of Parliament. "Who is there," he adds, "that
will take up the question of our white slave trade
with equal feeling?"

Three weeks later the problem had been solved.
On February 6th, 1833, the Rev. G. S. Bull, one of
the leaders in the movement, wrote to the Short
Time Committees: "I have succeeded, under Mr.
Sadler's sanction, in prevailing upon Lord Ashley
to move his (Mr. Sadler's) Bill."

It was not without a severe mental struggle that
Lord Ashley had arrived at this decision. He knew
absolutely nothing of the subject, he was even un-
aware that an inquiry into it had been instituted
by the House of Commons; he was only known in
the factory districts as having voted for benevolent
measures; his special aptitude and fitness for the task
had to be taken on trust. The task before him
was a gigantic one; and it was one of tremendous
self-denial. It meant the giving up of a political
career with its high offices, which, in the ordinary
course of things, seemed within his reach, and
turning his back on power, wealth, and comparative
ease, to throw himself into a fierce and long-
continuing warfare on behalf of the poor and the
oppressed. The task went farther still: to espouse
the factory cause was to give up home-comfort
and domestic leisure, to relinquish the scientific
and literary pursuits which had for him an intense

fascination—in short, to disturb the whole course of his natural life.

He was placed under the necessity of coming to an almost instantaneous decision, or a counter Bill would have been introduced by Lord Morpeth. He begged till next morning for consideration, took counsel of one or two friends, went home to seek guidance in prayer, and to lay the matter before his young wife. He painted in dark colours the sacrifices she would have to make, and the burden it would lay on her shoulders. Her name is embalmed by her answer. " It is your duty," she said, without hesitation ; " the consequences we must leave. Go forward, and to Victory ! "

On the following day Lord Ashley resolutely put his hand to the plough by giving notice in Parliament that he would move the re-introduction of the Ten Hours Bill. From the first his trumpet gave no uncertain sound ; he had taken up the measure as a matter of conscience, and as such he was determined to carry it through. His demands were : a period of ten hours for work and no more, the total abolition of night work, and eight hours only on Saturday. He declared that if the House would not adopt the Bill they must drive him from it, for he would not concede a step ; so long as he had a seat in that House, so long as God gave him health and a sound mind, he would spare no exertion, no effort of any kind, in and out of Parliament, to establish the success of the measure. He little knew that there lay before him fourteen years of incessant toil and struggle in this cause before he should obtain what he was striving for. He did not fully foresee that his strenuous activity would arouse corresponding resistance on the part of his opponents : he only knew for certain that it was his duty to persevere, and he persevered to the end.

From the first, too, he won the confidence of the operatives and of the many philanthropic men, such as the Rev. G. S. Bull, Mr. Sadler, Mr. Richard Oastler, Mr. Fielden, Mr. Brotherton, and others, who, with true-hearted enthusiasm, were pledged to the cause. " Had they not gone before," he wrote,* "and borne such an amount of responsibility and toil, I do not believe that it would have been in my power to have achieved anything at all."

The first campaign, and many subsequent ones, issued in defeat. The Government Bill (Lord Althorp's) was carried by an overwhelming majority ; and although it fell far short of what was desired, and would take effect slowly, it contained, nevertheless, some humane and highly useful provisions, and established for the first time the great principle that labour and education should be combined.

In order to give the new Act a fair trial, little was done for a few years in Parliament, but in 1838 the question was actively resumed by Lord Ashley. In the meantime, owing to the failure in enforcing the provisions of the Act, a persistent agitation had been maintained, and the brunt of the work

* "Speeches of the Earl of Shaftesbury, 1838—1867, upon Subjects having Relation chiefly to the Claims and Interests of the Working Classes" (London : Chapman & Hall, 1868), Preface, iv.

in correspondence and by personal appeal and interference had fallen to his lot.

In that year Mr. Poulett Thompson, M.P. for Manchester (afterwards Lord Sydenham), brought in a Bill to repeal a clause in Lord Althorp's Act, the effect of which would be to legalise the slavery of some forty thousand children whom the Government had solemnly pledged itself to protect. The factory districts were up in arms, stormy meetings were held, petitions were sent up to the House, and Lord Ashley moved that the Bill be read again that day six months. It was, however, pressed to a division; but in a House of 354 members it only secured a majority of two, and the Government thought it wise to withdraw the Bill.

On July 20th, 1838, Lord Ashley moved a resolution "That this House deeply regrets that the law affecting the regulation of the labour of children in factories, having been found imperfect and ineffective to the purposes for which it was passed, has been suffered to continue so long without any amendment." He supported the resolution in what has been described as one of the ablest speeches ever made on the Factory Question ; and denounced the Government in scathing terms on their dilatory conduct, pleading at the same time with intense earnestness for the 4,000,000 men, women, and children engaged in the various branches of cotton and other mills. Among many startling details he showed that out of 354,684 persons manually engaged in cotton mills 196,385 were females, being about

55 per cent., many mere children; and he had it on evidence that in 1832 the distance which a child travelled daily in the performance of its work was from twenty to twenty-five miles—"a severity of labour exceeding that imposed upon soldiers in forced marches, or under arms before the enemy"; that under the existing factory system as many died under twenty as elsewhere under forty; that the Act was daily violated with impunity, the educational clauses not being observed, the limit of hours not being adhered to, and that a generation was growing up totally ignorant of their rights as men and of their duties as Christians. He concluded with this powerful peroration :—

"Thus had a great measure, closely affecting the temporal and eternal welfare of so vast a portion of the population, been set aside and treated like a turnpike Bill. But the noble Lord * might be assured that the people of this country had too much humanity, and that he (Lord Ashley), who had humbly undertaken the subject, was too strongly determined to obtain justice to allow the matter to rest in its present state. Did he really think that he could stifle public sympathy, or silence him (Lord Ashley) by such devices? 'Though he should hold his peace, the very stones would immediately cry out.' . . . This evil, that was daily on the increase, was yet unremedied, though one-fifth part of the time the House had given to

* Lord John Russell.

the settlement of the question of negro slavery would have been sufficient to provide a remedy. When that House, in its wisdom and mercy, decided that forty-five hours in a week was a term of labour long enough for an adult negro, he thought it would not have been unbecoming that spirit of lenity if they had considered whether sixty-nine hours a week were not too many for the children of the British Empire. In the appeal he had now made he had asked nothing unreasonable, he had merely asked for an affirmation of a principle they had already recognised. He wanted them to decide whether they would amend, or repeal, or enforce, the Act now in existence. But if they would do none of these things, if they continued idly indifferent, and obstinately shut their eyes to this great and growing evil, if they would give no heed to that fierce and rapid cancer that was gnawing the very vitals of the social system, if they were careless of the growth of an immense population, plunged in ignorance and vice, which neither feared God nor regarded man, then he warned them that they must be prepared for the very worst results that could befall an empire." *

The resolution was lost in a division—121 voting for ministers and 106 against.

This division was too close to allow the Government to remain inactive, and in February of the following year they brought forward a Factory Act

* Hansard, Third Series, xliv. 113.

Amendment Bill. But it was a Bill only tinkering with the subject, and every proposal of Lord Ashley to improve it, so that it should be in some degree efficacious, was negatived. In the end, as he found it impossible to carry any of his points, he determined to oppose the measure altogether, and in consequence Lord John Russell withdrew the Bill, thereby paying a high tribute to the strength of Lord Ashley's position.

On March 31st, 1840, Lord Ashley moved for a Select Committee to inquire into the operation of the Act for the Regulation of Mills and Factories, which was agreed to without opposition.

While the Committee was pursuing its investigations he launched forth several other schemes for the amelioration of the condition of young people, notably for climbing boys (chimney sweeps), for children employed in mines and collieries, and for children in branches of trade and manufacture not included in the Factory Acts. To these we shall refer later on.

During the same period he made a tour in the cotton districts to put himself in personal communication with the various societies and to investigate the actual condition of the operatives. " I made it an invariable rule," he says, " to see everything with my own eyes ; to take nothing on trust or hearsay. In factories, I examined the mills, the machinery, the homes, and saw the workers and their work in all its details. In collieries, I went down into the pits. In London, I went into lodging-houses and thieves'

haunts, and every filthy place. It gave me a power
I could not otherwise have had. I could speak of
things from actual experience, and I used often to
hear things from the poor sufferers themselves which
were invaluable to me. I got to know their habits of
thought and action, and their actual wants. I sat and
had tea and talk with them hundreds of times." *

Lord Ashley had by this time become a recognised
power in the country. No one could fail to acknow-
ledge that he was possessed of far more than ordinary
talents for public business, and that these, combined
with social rank, which is no mean aid to political
success in England, would have raised him very high
in the official world. But the factory question stood
in the way. When, for example, Sir Robert Peel
formed his second Administration in 1841, he urgently
pressed upon Lord Ashley a place in it—whether
with a view to muzzle the agitating philanthropist or
whether as an honest recognition of his ability does
not matter here. His reply was a resolute refusal,
and the reasons for that refusal he explained in a
letter to one of the secretaries of the Short Time
Committees :—

" In answer to your inquiry on behalf of the operatives of the West Riding of Yorkshire, I have to reply
that an office was tendered to me by Sir Robert Peel.
Having, however, ascertained from him that his
opinions on the factory question were not matured,
and that he required further time for deliberation,

* " Life and Work," vol. i., p. 164.

I declined the acceptance of any place, under circumstances which would impede, or even limit, my full and free action in the advancement of that measure which I consider to be vital both to the welfare of the working classes and the real interests of the country. . . ."

This was not the only time he sacrificed his personal ambition to the cause he had at heart. Again and again Sir Robert Peel urged upon him the acceptance of office—at one time to occupy an important position in the Royal Household, at another (1845) to take the Chief Secretaryship of Ireland—but without avail. So late as 1866 Lord Derby offered him the Chancellorship of the Duchy of Lancaster and a seat in the Cabinet, but with the same result. " There were still remaining," he said, " fourteen hundred thousand women, children, and young persons to be brought under the protection of the Factory Acts," and till that was done he could not allow himself to be withdrawn from the great work of his life.

The change of Government in 1841 did not materially assist the cause of the operatives. Sir Robert Peel declined to support the Ten Hours Bill, and Sir James Graham, as Home Secretary, took the conduct of factory legislation into his own hands. In February 1844 he brought in his long-promised Bill for the Regulation of Labour in Factories. It proved to be totally inadequate, as it contained no education clauses and provided for twelve hours' labour. On February 12th it was read a second time

and ordered to be committed. Then commenced an
agitation outside such as had never been known in
the history of social reform, the watchword being,
"Ten Hours and No Surrender!" Meetings were
held, pamphlets scattered broadcast, members of
Parliament petitioned, and all the machinery of
agitation set in motion.

When the Bill went into Committee, Lord Ashley,
in a speech which occupied two hours and a quarter
in delivery, moved that the word "night" should be
understood as meaning from six o'clock in the evening
to six o'clock in the morning, thus practically limiting
the hours of labour to ten.   He began by saying :

" Nearly eleven years have now elapsed since I first
made the proposition to this House which I shall
renew this night.   Never at any time have I felt greater
apprehension or even anxiety ; not through any fear
of personal defeat, for disappointment is 'the badge
of all our tribe,' but because I know well the hostility
I have aroused, and the certain issues of indiscretion
on my part affecting the welfare of those who have so
long confided their hopes and interests to my charge."
Then, rebutting the charge that had so frequently
been made against him of being animated by a
peculiar animosity to factory employers, he showed,
in a masterly review, how the question had been dealt
with under every civilised form of government in
foreign countries.   He gave statistics and reports
from experts on practical labour, from medical men
on the physical mischiefs entailed, from merciful millowners who abhorred the system and waited for relief

from it, and from personal observation. He made startling revelations as to the appalling progress of female labour and its influence during the tenderest period of female life ; he verified previous statements he had made as to the nature of the work and the distances travelled during a day—statements which had been called in question ; and dwelt at large upon the Report of the Children's Employment Commission, "that awful document which excites a feeling of shame, terror, and indignation ! a fearful revelation of intemperance, impurity, demoralisation in every shape and form, and mainly attributable to the fact that wives and mothers and young daughters occupied the places in the factories that should have been filled with men."

"These sources of mischief," he cried vehemently, "must be dried up—every public consideration demands such an issue—the health of the females, the care of their families, their conjugal and parental duties, the comfort of their homes, the decency of their lives, the rights of their husbands, the peace of society, and the laws of God ; and, until a vote shall have been given this night—which God avert !—I never will believe that there can be found in this House one individual man who will deliberately and conscientiously inflict on the women of England such a burthen of insufferable toil . . .

"We ask but a slight relaxation of toil, a time to live and a time to die ; a time for those comforts that sweeten life, and a time for those duties that adorn it ; and therefore, with a fervent prayer to Almighty God that it may please Him to turn the hearts of all who hear me to thoughts of justice and of mercy, I now finally commit the issue to the judgment and humanity of Parliament." *

Unmoved by these appeals, Sir James Graham rose and announced the intention of Government to give the proposition their emphatic opposition, while John Bright, in a violent speech, declared that there was not any need for a new Factory Act, and made a series of charges against Lord Ashley, for which he was called upon to apologise, the " scene " which ensued being memorable in Parliamentary annals.

Had the House divided that night there is little doubt that the Government would have been defeated ; but the debate was adjourned.   On its resumption, Sir Robert Peel, in the course of a long speech, "ingenious in argument, but wretched in principle," asked why other branches of trade and manufacture should not have the same privileges sought by those included in the Factories Bill, and concluded by asking, " Is the House prepared to legislate for all these people ? "   To his surprise and mortification a ringing cry of " Yes," with long resounding cheers, was the reply.   " Then," said he in angry tones, " I see not why we should not extend the restriction to agriculture."   Another tremendous cheer broke forth in acquiescence, and, dumfounded, he sat down, saying in conclusion, " I cannot and I *will not* acquiesce in the proposal of the noble lord."

* Hansard, Third Series, lxx. 483.

Two divisions were taken : the result, a majority of eight in favour of Lord Ashley's proposition.

Already Sir James Graham had endeavoured by a stratagem to rescind the votes, and he determined to make another attempt. Rising amid a solemn silence, he said, " Sir, the decision of the Committee is a virtual adoption of a Ten Hours Bill without modification. To that decision, with the utmost respect for the opinion of the Committee, I have an insuperable objection."

The Government determined to try over again the whole question by a division on the following Friday, thus giving themselves an opportunity of employing every Government method of influence and coercion. This further stratagem succeeded ; the voting was thrown into hopeless confusion by again taking two votes ; the Government Bill for Twelve Hours and Lord Ashley's Bill for Ten Hours were both negatived, and progress was reported !

A compromise, in the shape of an Eleven Hours Bill, would have at this time been accepted by Lord Ashley, reserving to himself the power of moving when he pleased ; but Sir James Graham was resolved to stick to the Twelve Hours—and notwithstanding the popular outcry, and a memorial to the Queen from all the Committees, he brought forward a new Bill. Just on the eve of victory, as it seemed, this decision was very painful to Lord Ashley. He sought rest and quiet, if only for a few days, until the attack should be renewed. But it was in vain. " I am haunted," he wrote, " and I know I shall be haunted by debates, divisions, spectres of attacks, failure, success." He was of a nervous and excitable temperament, and the constant, unrelieved strain, not only of the Factory Question, but of many others, almost, if not quite, as important, was more than he could sustain.

On May 3rd, 1844, Graham's new Bill was brought forward, and was so worded that it would not admit of any amendment being proposed on any of its clauses, and Lord Ashley was obliged to give notice that he would move the introduction of a new clause —viz., " That no young person should be employed more than eleven hours a day, or sixty-four hours a week ; and that from October 1st, 1847, these numbers should be reduced to ten hours a day, or fifty-eight hours a week."

The interval was one of great mental trial. " I am certainly conscious of a decline in physical and mental energy," he wrote ; " I have no sense of comfort from above ; I have seen no pillar of cloud by day, or of fire by night ; my spirits do not rally. . . . I am languid, weary, diffident ; many assail and no one defends me. . . . I never felt so forlorn as I do now."

But by May 10th, when he rose to move the introduction of the new clause, all his old strength and courage had apparently returned. For cogency of argument, for vigorous denunciation, for depth of feeling in pleading for justice and humanity, his speech could not have been better. " We have at last lighted such a candle in England as, by God's blessing, shall never be put out," he cried, as he sat down amid vociferous cheers.

The effect upon Sir James Graham was paralysing —he could not answer the convincing arguments he had heard; he felt that the crisis of the Ministry had come, and after a short preamble, in which he paid a tribute to the high motives of Lord Ashley, concluded thus : " I must say, with perfect submission and perfect frankness, that I leave this case to the decision of the House ; but, with equal firmness and with equal frankness, I am bound to state that if the decision of the House should be that the proposition of the noble lord should prevail, it will be my duty to seek a private station, hoping that the decision of the House may be conducive to the welfare of the country." The debate was adjourned ; and on its resumption, three days later, Sir Robert Peel concluded a two hours' speech by saying, " I know not what the result may be this night, but this I do know, that I shall with a safe conscience, if the result be unfavourable to my views, retire with perfect satisfaction into a private station, wishing well to the result of your legislation."

There could be but one outcome of this malevolent action on the part of the Ministry : the vote would be to save the Government—not against the Ten Hours Bill. And so it proved. Ayes, 159 ; Noes, 297. Majority against Lord Ashley's amendment, 138 !!

Next day he wrote : " Last night defeated—utterly, singularly, prodigiously defeated by a majority of 138 ! The House seemed aghast, perplexed, astounded.

No one could say how, why, and almost *when*. It seemed that 35 or 40 was the highest majority expected. Such is the power and such the exercise of ministerial influence !"

The Bill, which, be it remembered, was a distinct gain to the operatives, inasmuch as it established the principle that adult female labour should be restricted, was strongly opposed by Lord Brougham on the third reading, but without avail, and on June 6th, 1844, it became law.

A brief but vivid description of the public and political excitement of the time is given in Greville's "Journal," * which we quote here with pleasure, as it emanates from one who had no great sympathy with either the operatives or with the philanthropists who were working for them.   He says :—

"I never remember so much excitement as has been caused by Ashley's Ten Hours Bill, nor a more curious state of things—such intermingling of parties, such a confusion of opposition ; a question so much more open than any question ever was before, and yet not made so or acknowledged to be so with the Government ; so much zeal, asperity, and animosity ; so many reproaches hurled backwards and forwards. The Government have brought forward their measure in a very positive way, and have clung to it with great tenacity, rejecting all compromise ; they have been abandoned by nearly half their supporters, and

* "Journal of the Reign of Queen Victoria, 1837—1852," by C. C. Greville, vol. ii., p. 230.

nothing can exceed their chagrin and disappointment at being so forsaken. Some of them attribute it to Graham's unpopularity, and aver that if Peel had brought it forward, or if a meeting had been previously called, they would not have been defeated; again, some declare that Graham had said they were indifferent to the result, and that people might vote as they pleased, which he stoutly denies. Then John Russell, voting for 'Ten Hours,' against all he professed last year, has filled the world with amazement and many of his own friends with indignation. It has, I think, not redounded to his credit, but, on the contrary, done him considerable harm. The Opposition were divided—Palmerston and Lord John one way, Baring and Labouchere the other. It has been a very queer affair. Some voted, not knowing how they ought to vote, and following those they are accustomed to follow. Many who voted against Government afterwards said they believed they were wrong. Melbourne is all against Ashley; all the political economists, of course; Lord Spencer strong against him. Then Graham gave the greatest offence by taking up a word of the *Examiner* of last Sunday, and calling it a 'Jack Cade legislation,' this stirring them to fury, and they flew upon him like tigers. Ashley made a speech as violent and factious as any of O'Connell's, and old Inglis was overflowing with wrath. . . . Lyndhurst rubbed his hands with great glee, and said, ' Well, we shall hear no more of "aliens" now; people will only talk of "Jack Cade" for the future,' too happy to shift the odium, if he could, from his own to his colleague's back. The ministers gave out, if they were beaten last Friday, they would resign ; but they knew there was no chance of it. Some abused Ashley for not going on and fighting again, but he knew well enough it would be of no use. The House did certainly put itself in an odd predicament, with its two votes directly opposed to each other. The whole thing is difficult and unpleasant. Government will carry their Bill now, and Ashley will be able to do nothing, but he will go on agitating session after session ; and a philanthropic agitator is more dangerous than a repealer, either of the Union or the Corn Laws. We are just now overrun with philanthropy, and God knows where it will stop or whither it will lead us."

What Lord Ashley had gained up to this period on behalf of the operatives was not inconsiderable : an enactment limiting the labour of children to six hours a day ; protection against accident, death, and mutilation from the unguarded state of the machinery ; and the important provision that no woman, of whatever age, should be employed in any mill or factory more than twelve hours a day.

He urged upon all the various Committees to give the new Bill a fair and patient trial, and he was determined to fortify himself with fresh arguments to be gained from frequent visits to the factory districts. But, in the summer of 1845, a cloud no bigger than a man's hand appeared on the horizon, and it spread rapidly till it covered all the sky.

Disease had fallen on the potato crops. It was prevalent throughout Kent and Sussex; it might spread to Ireland, as in fact it did; and that meant ruin and starvation, the people being largely dependent on potatoes for their daily sustenance. Sir Robert Peel, who was pledged to maintain the Corn Laws, came to the conclusion that he could no longer do so; the existing duties must be at once suspended, and the ports thrown open to the importation of provisions of every kind; and accordingly he resigned his seat. Lord John Russell, who had become a convert to the principles of the Anti-Corn Law League, was summoned to form a Government, but failing, Sir Robert Peel was reinstated.

It was at this critical juncture that Lord Ashley, as we have seen,* constrained by conscience and encouraged by his noble wife, resigned his seat in Parliament in justice to his constituents, to whom he, too, was pledged to maintain the Corn Laws.

Two days before doing so (June 29th, 1846) he again moved to bring in his Ten Hours Bill, and in a vigorous speech brought forward a mass of evidence to show that the reduction of hours of labour had acted beneficially: the produce was not diminished; the work was better done, as the workers were in better spirits; the operatives were in better health; the attendance at night schools had risen 25 per cent.; the taste for reading was growing among the work-people, and many large millowners testified that the

* See p. 17.

change had resulted in their profit and advantage. The Bill was read a first time; and two days afterwards, Lord Ashley being no longer a member of Parliament, the charge of the Bill was undertaken by one of the staunchest adherents to its principles, Mr. Fielden, the member for Oldham.

Out of Parliament Lord Ashley's exertions were ceaseless in the factory districts; his movements were, as he said, "like the pertinacious, unwearied revolution of a steam engine." But he came back to London to be present in the lobby—for he had not the heart to attend under the gallery—at the second reading, the debate lasting for the whole day. Two adjournments were made, and on May 22nd the Bill was lost by a majority of ten.

A month later Sir Robert Peel was defeated on the Irish Coercion Bill, greatly to the delight of Lord Ashley, and Lord John Russell, now the staunch friend of factory legislation, came into power.

It was not, however, till January in 1847 that Mr. Fielden brought in the Bill again. Lord Ashley was still out of Parliament, but he lingered about the House of Commons while the Bill was under discussion, nervously anxious to take his part in it, and grieving at his inability to do so. " I dream of it by day and night," he wrote, " and work as though I had charge of the Bill."

On May 3rd the Bill was carried by a majority of sixty-three, and on June 1st it successfully passed its final stage. On that day Lord Ashley wrote in his diary :—

"*June* 1st. Six o'clock. News that the Factory Bill has just passed the third reading. I am humbled that my heart is not bursting with thankfulness to Almighty God—that I can find breath and sense to express my joy. What reward shall we give unto the Lord for all the benefits He hath conferred upon us? God, in His mercy, prosper the work, and grant that these operatives may receive the cup of Salvation and call upon the name of the Lord! Praised be the Lord! Praised be the Lord in Christ Jesus!"

So ended the fourteen years' battle on behalf of the poor women and children who had been ground down in the slavery of the cotton mills, and the great victory was hailed throughout the country with intense enthusiasm. There was, however, much to be done to guard the protection that had been so laboriously won; and Lord Ashley, having been in the meantime returned for Bath—" without asking a single vote or paying a single farthing," to the discomfiture of his bitter opponent, Mr. Roebuck, was able in his own person to head another fight for the cause.

It was still legal to run the mills for fifteen hours a day—*i.e.*, from 5.30 a.m. to 8.30 p.m.—and it became the practice of many owners to divide their female and young hands into relays and shifts so as to keep the machinery going the whole of the time. " The result was that the limitation of the protected labour to ten hours daily was evaded in reality, without any literal infringement of the law which could be easily detected; for the hands were detained in the works the whole fifteen hours at a stretch, so as to be always ready to take up their turns, and it became impossible for the inspectors to discover and convict of a serious imposition of overtime. The legality of the system of shifts was tested in the Law Courts, but in vain ; it was upheld, and fresh legislation was the only alternative." Accordingly, in 1850, Lord Ashley introduced a new Bill to meet the emergency, and, after several attempts at a compromise, the settlement was reached that the working day for women and children, which by the Act of 1847 was commenced at 5.30 a.m. and continued to 8.30 p.m., was fixed to begin at 6 a.m. and end at 6 p.m., with an hour and a half for meals —that is to say ten and a half hours of labour daily— with the exception of Saturdays, on which no protected person should be allowed to work after 2 p.m. Thus the result was a Ten Hours and a Half law with the modification of a half-holiday on Saturday. This compromise, which was unpopular and produced a storm of disapproval at first, continued in force till 1878, when Mr. Cross (now Lord Cross), in consolidating the Factory Laws, reduced the hours of labour to ten.

We must not lose sight of the exceptional difficulties Lord Ashley had to contend with throughout this long struggle. Bodies of men organised for the special purpose of agitating for reform, are not, as a rule, capable of easy management. It was necessary to conciliate the millowners on the one hand and on the other to encourage the workpeople. " Soft sawder to the millowners," he said, " is a damper to the men ; and a stirrer to the men is a damper to the

millowners." Nevertheless, he was singularly successful with both. He had laid down at the outset a few
simple rules to govern the conduct of the movement,
and he never lost an opportunity of enforcing them.
It was agreed " that the proceedings should be carried
on in the most conciliatory manner ; that there should
be a careful abstinence from all approach to questions
of wages and capital ; that the labour of children and
young persons should alone be touched ; that there
should be no strikes, no intimidation, and no strong
language against their employers " ; * and many years
later from his place in Parliament he was able to
say of himself, " I have carefully abstained, both here
and among the people themselves, from all exciting
language ; I have studied to produce and to maintain
a good understanding between the employer and the
employed ; I have never ceased to exhort those who
confided this measure to my charge, that their thoughts,
their feelings, and their actions must be brought under
the dominion of self-control. Well, sir, I rejoice to
say that the effort has been successful. I might have
resorted to other means, and kept up their zeal by
every inflammatory topic. . . . I might have collected
them, not by hundreds but by thousands, and talked
to them of their wrongs and their rights, of where
submission ends and where resistance begins ; but I
have done no such thing ; and I may now say, to the
high honour of those who have so long and so patiently
sustained this conflict, that I have never witnessed one

* " Shaftesbury's Speeches," Preface, iv.

menacing effort, or heard from them one vindictive expression." *

Perhaps there is nothing more interesting in the whole history of social reform than the persistency of this one man who, amid the deadliest opposition and the bitterest hatred, held on his way until he had accomplished his task, and not only won his way into general favour, but gained the admiration of his most formidable antagonists.

Mr. Roebuck, who had opposed him tooth and nail with rancorous bitterness, publicly recanted his sentiments in Parliament, and declared that the views which prompted his action had been wrong in almost every particular.† "The evidence supplied by the enactments which you promoted," he wrote to Lord Shaftesbury, "made a convert of me, and led me, as far as I was able, to imitate your example and follow in your footsteps."

Sir James Graham, for whom there was some excuse, seeing that men in responsible offices naturally hesitate to incur the risk of deranging the labour market and of driving industry to other countries, made a confession in Parliament, saying that his former evil predictions had not been verified by the result, and nobly added, " That great measure of relief for women and children has contributed to the well-being and comfort of the working classes, whilst it has not injured their masters. . . . By the vote I shall give to-night I will endeavour to make some amends for

* "Shaftesbury's Speeches," p. 211.
† *Times*, March 22nd, 1860.

the course I pursued in earlier life in opposing the Factory Bill." *

Mr. Gladstone ever voted in resistance to Lord Ashley's efforts, but in 1864 he partially retracted by saying, with reference to interference by prohibition in the Factory Acts : " It is an interference, as to which it may be said that the Legislature is now almost unanimous with respect to the necessity which existed for undertaking it, and with respect to the beneficial effect it has produced, both in mitigating human suffering and in attaching important classes of the community to Parliament and the Government."

Richard Cobden, though bitterly hostile in the early days of Factory Legislation, abstained from opposition to other movements and gave positive support to some.

Lord John Russell, though at first out of sympathy with the cause, afterwards espoused it with great vigour, while Sir George Grey and Lord Macaulay manfully gave in their adherence. O'Connell, Lord Brougham, and John Bright were from first to last bitter opponents.

It may be mentioned here, and should be borne in mind when considering the whole of Lord Shaftesbury's life, that he was never a rich man ; on the contrary, for a man of his position and influence, he was positively poor. His estrangement from his father, who disapproved of the course in

* *Times*, May 9th, 1860.

political life he had marked out for himself, or, as he would say, "God had clearly marked out for him," was a material loss, no less than a great heart trouble. Throughout his diaries we find frequent complaints of the pressure on his purse, the lowness of his finances, and sometimes of positive embarrassments, which made it difficult for him to carry on his work, and prevented him from helping others according to the dictates of his heart. Let one entry suffice :—

"*Dec.* 31*st*, 1846. Crœsus would be pauperised if he were to meet half the demands that are made upon me every month! Alas! I must refuse the largest proportion and give very sparingly to the remainder. I say 'alas' because the cases are often-times meritorious, and I shall always be misrepresented, and frequently misunderstood. Many people choose to believe that I am rich, and ask accordingly; yet more than half of my income is borrowed, to be repaid at some future day with heavy accumulations of interest; eight children, the two eldest costing me more than £200 a year each; a ninth coming, and an allowance from my father of only £100 annually more than I had as a bachelor at Oxford." *

In the light of this statement we see more vividly than ever how great was the self-sacrifice involved in the persistent refusal of high offices in the State with their corresponding emolument.

* "Life and Work," etc. vol. ii., p. 187.

On June 2nd, 1851, his father died at the age of eighty-three, and Lord Ashley, then fifty years of age, succeeded to the title and estates. But this change increased, rather than alleviated, his financial embarrassments. He found the estate in a sadly neglected condition, the cottages "close, indecent, unwholesome." "And what can I do?" he asked himself. "I am half pauperised; the debts are endless; no money is payable for a whole year, and I am not a young man. Every sixpence I expend—and spend I must on many things—is *borrowed*." For a quarter of a century those debts haunted him, dogged his steps, oppressed him like a nightmare; and it was only after a desperate struggle, by small sales of outlying property, by disposal of tithes to the Ecclesiastical Commissioners, and other devices, that he paid off at last the ruinous mortgage on the St. Giles estate.

CHAPTER III

LUNATICS, AND THE LUNACY LAWS.

Hansard
3rd Series
lxvi
1257

THE first speech Lord Ashley ever delivered in Parliament was on February 19th, 1828, when he seconded a motion of Mr. Robert Gordon for " A Bill to amend the Law for the Regulation of Lunatic Asylums." It was a subject on which his compassion had been for some time expended, and it was one which needed, almost more than any other at that time, thorough investigation, with a view to check the evils crying aloud for redress.

The barbarous treatment of lunatics even so recently as the latter part of the last century and the first quarter of the present century is almost incredible to-day. Although in some places asylums were provided, the system pursued was almost invariably coercion, severity, and cruelty. Up to the year 1771, for example, the lunatics in the old Hospital of Bethlem, in Moorfields, London, were exhibited for a fee of twopence, as if they had been wild beasts, and the poor creatures were goaded to fury, to render the exhibition more exciting. In the year when this shameful exhibition was prohibited, Henry Mackenzie published his " Man of Feeling," containing a description of the hospital. " Their conductor," he says, " led them first to the dismal mansions of those who are in the most horrible state of incurable madness. The clanking of chains, the wildness of their cries, and the imprecations which some of them uttered, formed a scene inexpressibly shocking. Harley and his companions, especially the female part of them, begged their guide to return ; he seemed surprised at their uneasiness, and was with difficulty prevailed on to leave that part of the house without showing them some others, who, as he expressed it, in the phrase of those that keep wild beasts for show, were much better worth seeing than any they had passed, being ten times more fierce and unmanageable." Mackenzie puts into the mouth of Harley words which express the dawning of new opinion, no less than the ignorance of the times. " I think it an inhuman practice," he says, " to expose the greatest misery with which our race is afflicted, to every idle visitant who can afford a trifling perquisite to the keeper ; especially as it is a distress which the humane must see with the painful reflection that it is not in their power to alleviate it."

It will be remembered that the last picture in Hogarth's series of " The Rake's Progress " gives even a more vivid scene of a madhouse of the period. Nearly naked, in chains, his head shaved, in a dark, dirty, straw-littered cell, and wildly raging, the poor maniac is being exhibited by his brutal-looking keeper.

In 1774 the first law relating to the "proper" treatment of pauper lunatics was passed, and that merely authorised any two Justices to apprehend them and have them locked up and chained. There was not at that time in this country any conception of humane and kindly treatment for insane persons, nor had medical science sufficiently advanced to form any notion of curative measures. Insanity was regarded as hopeless ; the sufferer was to be chained, restrained, whipped, and left in a dark cell under the charge of a "keeper," to sink into a state of mere brutality.

M. Philippe Pinel, a French physician, was the first to attempt the restoration of the insane to a position among human beings. In 1792 he obtained permission from the Government to unloose a certain number of maniacs detained in the Bicêtre, a hospital near Paris for insane men, and try upon them the effects of mild treatment. The first case he selected was that of an English captain who had been chained in a dark, unwarmed, and unventilated cell for nearly forty years, and who, in a fit of fury, had killed one of his keepers with a blow from his manacles. The effect of Pinel's treatment was surprising. The patient gave his word of honour that if set free he would not injure any one. He kept his word, had no return of his previous paroxysms, and for two years afterwards rendered himself useful in the hospital by exercising a kind of authority over other insane patients.*

Unhappily, no Pinel had arisen in this country, nor

* *British and Foreign Medical Review.*

was it till nearly twenty years later that any active public steps were taken to establish a humane system of treatment.

"In the early part of the present century," says Mr. Robert Gardiner Hill,* "lunatics were kept constantly chained to walls in dark cells, and had nothing to lie upon but straw. The keepers visited them, whip in hand, and lashed them into obedience. They were also half drowned in 'baths of surprise,' and in some cases semi-strangulation was resorted to. The 'baths of surprise' were so constructed that the patients in passing over a trap-door fell in ; some patients were chained in wells, and the water made to rise until it reached their chins. One horrible contrivance was a rotatory chair, in which patients were made to sit and were revolved at a frightful speed. The chair was in common use. Patients, women as well as men, were flogged at particular periods, chained and fastened to iron bars, and even confined in iron cages."

So late as 1815—that is to say, when Lord Ashley was a boy of fourteen years of age—there might have been seen in Bethlem a patient, once an officer in the navy, for whose "benefit" a new instrument of torture had been invented. "A stout iron ring was riveted round his neck, from which a short chain passed to a ring made to slide upwards or downwards on an upright, massive iron bar, more than six feet high,

* "Lunacy: Its Past and its Present," by Robert Gardiner Hill, F.S.A., p. 1.

inserted into the wall. Round his body a strong iron bar about two inches wide was riveted; on each side of the bar was a circular projection, which, being fashioned to and enclosing each of his arms, pinioned them close to his sides. The waist-bar was secured by two similar bars, which, passing over his shoulders, were riveted to the waist-bar both before and behind. The iron ring round his neck was connected to his shoulders by a double link. From each of these bars another chain passed to the ring on the upright iron bar. His right leg was chained to the trough, in which he had remained thus encaged and enchained twelve years. He read books of all kinds, and reasoned quite coherently on the events of the war." During the whole of this period it was impossible for him, from the nature of his restraint, to stand quite upright, or to lie down at ease. He died in 1815, the year in which a Committee of Inquiry into the State of English Madhouses issued their report —a revelation of such frightful abuses, of such brutality and profligacy of keepers, of such wanton cruelty and hopeless suffering, that it is quite unfit to quote in any detail here. For those who wish to pursue the subject there is ample record in the works of the pioneers of more enlightened treatment.*

From this date, very slowly, it is true, improvement in the condition of the insane may be traced; larger asylums were opened, leather chains were substituted

* See particularly " History of the Insane in the British Isles," by D. Hack Tuke, M.D., and Mr. Hill's work already referred to.

for iron ones, some attention was paid to warming and clothing, and an attempt at proper inspection by magistrates was made.

But no really earnest and effectual steps were taken to remedy this gigantic evil until 1828, when Lord Ashley seconded Mr. Gordon's motion for "A Bill to Amend the Law for the Regulation of Lunatic Asylums." It was but a poor speech he made on that occasion, spoken "in so low a tone," says Hansard, "that it was nearly inaudible in the gallery," and referred to by himself in these words: "Last night I ventured to speak, and, God be praised, I did not utterly disgrace myself, though the exhibition was far from glorious." It was a speech, however, that will always have a historical interest, for it launched him forth in his career of social reform. "By God's blessing," he said, "my first effort has been for the advancement of human happiness. May I improve hourly!"

The Bill passed into law, transferring the power over lunatics from the College of Physicians to a Board of Commissioners in Lunacy, fifteen in number. Lord Ashley was chosen as one of these, and in the following year became chairman, a post which he retained throughout his long life, with the exception of a very short period in the year before his death, when he resigned on account of his disapproval of Lord Selborne's Lunacy Bill. The Bill, however, fell through, and Lord Shaftesbury was able to resume his position.

In this connection it may be mentioned that shortly

after his death a correspondent of the *Times* (John Charles Bricknill) wrote to call attention to Lord Shaftesbury as an official, "an important phase in his life, which would seem to have been somewhat disregarded under the brighter light shed upon his memory by his extraordinary philanthropic work. . . . Yet Lord Shaftesbury was one of the oldest and one of the most painstaking of English officials, to the day of his death presiding over an important department of the public service, as Chairman of the Commissioners in Lunacy, an office which he had held virtually for about fifty-eight years; an office the delicate and difficult duties of which he discharged with admirable knowledge, judgment, and assiduity . . . but for which Lord Shaftesbury never received one farthing of pecuniary reward; and it is much to be feared that he received no amount even of gratitude at all commensurate with his services."

It was not until several years later than 1828 that any further important steps were taken towards improvement; but in the meantime Lord Ashley made visits of inspection to many asylums in London and the provinces, and saw such horrible sights and learnt such painful lessons of "man's inhumanity to man" that he "vowed he would never cease pleading the cause of these poor creatures till either death silenced him or the laws were amended."

He found his duties in the Commission painful and onerous. It was an unpleasant and responsible office either to detain or discharge a patient, as in the one case there was the hazard of cruelty to the prisoner, and in the other to his friends or the public. In one instance a violent, coarse, and heartless ruffian was incarcerated ; but there was no proof of personal violence against him, and upon a division of six to four—the first division that had taken place in ten years—the man was set at liberty. "A decision on our part that he was rightfully detained," said Lord Ashley, "would have authorised the incarceration in a Bedlam of seven-tenths of the human race who have ever been excited to violence of speech and gesture."

This difficulty so pressed upon Lord Ashley, more particularly when a Bill, brought in by Lord Granville Somerset, passed into law in 1842 extending the powers of the Board of Commissioners to the provinces, that in 1844, the year before the statute under which they acted would expire, he ventilated the subject in Parliament. Before doing so he prepared an elaborate report containing the result of the investigations of the Commissioners into the state of Lunatic Asylums generally—a report so comprehensive that it has been called "the Domesday Book of all that, up to that time, concerned institutions for the insane." It was a terrible revelation of distressing facts, almost too painful to read, but it led to beneficial legislation, the effects of which are now patent to every one.

On moving for an address to the Crown, praying Her Majesty to take into her consideration this Report of the Metropolitan Commissioners in Lunacy, Lord Ashley contended that it was the duty of the House to prescribe the conditions under which a man should be deprived of his liberty, and also those under which he might be released ; it was their duty to take care that for those who required restraint there should be provided kind and competent keepers, and that, while the patient received no injury, the public should be protected.

There were at that time three classes of accommodation for the insane : they were lodged either in single or private dwelling-houses, in public or county asylums, or in private asylums where paupers were also received. In regard to the first class the Commissioners had no power to interfere, and Lord Ashley was of opinion that even in private families a power of this kind ought to be confided to some hands that would hunt out and expose the many horrible abuses that then prevailed. There were many patients in these single houses for whom was paid not less than £500 per annum, and this was a temptation to keep such a patient in perpetual confinement, because with the returning health of the sufferer the allowance would be discontinued. So strong was his opinion of the bad effect of this that " if," said he, " Providence should afflict any near relative of mine with insanity, I would consign him to an asylum in which there were other patients, and which was subject to official visitation." The only attempt at a safeguard to abuse was that if the patient resided in the house over a twelvemonth, the owner of the house was bound to communicate the name of that patient to the Commissioners. This, however, was easily evaded by several devices, one being to remove the patient after a residence of eleven months to some other lodging.

The second class of accommodation was the county asylum. Many of these were quite unfit for the reception of insane persons; others were suitable according to the feeling of the times, and were in all respects well conducted; but twenty-one counties in England and Wales were without any asylum whatever, either public or private. All the public asylums then in existence had the advantage of constant supervision and of not giving any profit to the superintendents, so that it was not necessary that the keeper should stint and spare his patients in the articles necessary for the curative process, with the view of realising a profit.

The third class was that of private asylums, which received persons who paid their own expenses, and also paupers. In these houses horrible abuses existed, paupers being sent there to be maintained at the low rate of 7s. or 8s. a week, "out of which the proprietor was to feed, and clothe, and house the patient, and carry on the remedial process, paying all these expenses and still getting a profit." Many instances were quoted by Lord Ashley showing the disgusting condition in which some of these asylums were found to be. We give one example only, and that of the mildest type :—

" West Auckland.—Thirteen males, sixteen females ; the violent and the quiet, the dirty and the clean, shut up together ; only one small yard, and when the one sex was in it the other shut up ; in the day room of the males five restrained by leg-locks, and two wearing, in addition, iron handcuffs and fetters from the wrist to the ankle.   All tranquil, but they would otherwise escape.   Chains fastened to floor in many places, and to many of the bedsteads.   The males throughout the house slept two in a bed."

In the course of his speech Lord Ashley strongly emphasised the great benefit, as well as great saving of expense, that resulted from the application of curative means at an early stage of insanity, and urged that it was the duty of the State to provide receptacles for the incurable patients apart from those devoted to the remedial treatment.   He paid a high tribute to those good and able men, Mr. Tuke, Dr. Hitch, Dr. Corsellis, Dr. Conolly, Dr. Vitré, Dr. Charlesworth, and others, " who had brought all their high moral and intellectual qualities to bear on the subject, and had laboured to make the rational and humane treatment to be the rule and principle of the government of lunacy."   He instanced a striking experience which, true in those days, would be found to be even more so in these—viz., the fact " that no more frequent cause of insanity existed than was found in intoxication ; the number of persons who were confined in lunatic asylums, and whose insanity originated in drunkenness, was very great, and would surprise any person who was not aware of the effects of this habit."   He deprecated in strong language the confinement of criminal lunatics in private asylums, and asked the House whether it was not an improper and unnecessary aggravation of their miseries towards the other lunatics to subject them to confinement in the same place and under the same regulations as criminals, such regulations being more severe than elsewhere, and debarring them from much indulgence which, under other circumstances, their melancholy position would have procured for them.

Lord Ashley concluded his remarkable speech in these words :—

" These unhappy persons [lunatics generally] are outcasts from all the social and domestic affections of private life—nay, more, from all its cares and duties—and have no refuge but in the laws. You can prevent, by the agency you shall appoint, as you have in many instances prevented, the recurrence of frightful cruelties ; you can soothe the days of the incurable, and restore many sufferers to health and usefulness. For we must not run away with the notion that even the hopelessly mad are dead to all capacity of intellectual or moral exertion—quite the reverse ; their feelings, too, are painfully alive— I have seen them writhe under supposed contempt, while a word of kindness and respect would kindle their whole countenance into an expression of joy. Their condition appeals to our highest sympathies,

" 'Majestic, though in ruin,'

for though there may be, in the order of a merciful Providence, some compensating dispensation which abates within, the horrors manifested without, we must judge alone by what we see; and I trust, therefore, that I shall stand excused, though I have consumed so much of your valuable time, when you call to mind that this motion is made on behalf of the most helpless, if not the most afflicted portion, of the human race." *

Here the matter rested for a year; but on June 6th, 1845, Lord Ashley brought in, at the request of the Government, two Bills of such an inclusive and exhaustive nature that scarcely an evil of any kind capable of remedy was left untouched. One Bill was "For the Regulation of Lunatic Asylums," and the other "For the better Care and Treatment of Lunatics in England and Wales."

It would be wearisome to give in this place even the outlines of Lord Ashley's speech in bringing forward these Bills, which were to affect the repeal of many existing Acts respecting the treatment of lunatics and to substitute such other enactments in their places as time, circumstances, and extended knowledge had rendered necessary. Speaking broadly, the Bills provided for competent and more frequent inspection of all asylums; the placing of them under humane and therefore proper regulations; they fixed the limit of expenses, gave power to the Chancellor to protect the property of lunatics, made the erection of county asylums compulsory, and provided for the prompt care and treatment of all classes of lunatics on the development of their insanity.

* Hansard, Third Series, lxxvi. 1257

There was no opposition in the debate that followed, the concluding words of Lord Ashley's speech having produced a palpable effect :—

"Here are we," he said, "sitting in deliberation to-day ; to-morrow we may be subjects of this fearful affliction. Causes, as slight, apparently, as they are sudden, varying through every degree of intensity— a fall, a fever, a reverse of fortune, a domestic calamity —will do the awful work, and then ' Farewell, King ! ' The most exalted intellects, the noblest affections, are transformed into fatuity and corruption, and leave nothing but the sad, though salutary lesson— how frail is the tenure by which we hold all that is precious and dignified in human nature." *

The two Bills passed into law in that same year, and they have been rightly designated "The Magna Charta of the Liberties of the Insane."

A permanent Lunacy Commission of competent men, whose functions were greatly widened, was now introduced, six of them receiving salaries of £1,500 each, while Lord Ashley, one of the hardest workers from the beginning, became once more *unpaid* chairman of the Commission, an office, as we have already seen, that he retained to the end of his life. For many long years this heavy and responsible work occupied a very large portion of his time and energy. He would see into cases himself, and not be content with second-hand

* Hansard, Third Series, lxxxi. 180.

information.   Let one illustration of his activity, even
late in life, suffice :—

"A lady, Mrs. A., residing in the West End, was
on visiting terms with Mrs. B., a woman of fashion
and position.   There was little in common between the
two, and the visits of Mrs. A. would have been less
frequent than they were, had she not taken a more
than passing interest in a young lady, Miss C., who
was staying, indefinitely as it seemed, in the house
of Mrs. B.   There was a great charm in her conversa-
tion, and the visits of Mrs. A. seemed to afford her
considerable pleasure, though they were only of an
occasional and somewhat formal kind.   One day
when Mrs. A. called, Miss C. was not there, and on
making very pointed inquiries, she was, after some
hesitation, informed that her young friend was out of
her mind and was in an asylum fifty miles away from
town, the name of the asylum being mentioned.

"That evening Mrs. A. felt troubled and distressed:
she had seen Miss C. only a week or ten days previously, and perceived no indication of a disordered
mind.   It was true she had observed indications
of sadness and depression of spirits, and had feared
that her young friend was not happy ; but that she
was out of her mind, and fit to be in an asylum, she
could not and would not believe.   She was greatly
troubled, not knowing what to do or where to go.
At length it occurred to her that the Earl of Shaftesbury was a Commissioner in Lunacy, and she went
straight away to his house, found him at home, and
told him the whole story.   It was evening when she

arrived in Grosvenor Square, and dinner was on the table, but within a quarter of an hour Lord Shaftesbury was on his way to the railway station to go down to the asylum and investigate the matter for himself. He did so, and on the following day the young lady was released, it having been authoritatively ascertained that she was not in a state to render it necessary for her to be an inmate of an asylum." *

In 1852, the year after Lord Ashley had become Earl of Shaftesbury, he brought before the House of Lords the question of criminal lunatics, with a view to the erection of a State asylum for this class, whose incarceration in other asylums was prejudicial to the inmates, and checked the operation of the system of non-restraint—"a system, the great and blessed glory of modern science, which, by the blessing of God, had achieved miracles." † Nothing further was done at that time, but the promise of Lord Derby was given that the subject should not be lost sight of, and in 1860 the Act was passed which resulted in the erection of the State Criminal Asylum at Broadmoor.

About the same period (1861) Lord Shaftesbury busied himself in an effort to establish a Benevolent Asylum for the Insane of the Middle Classes, where, upon payment of reasonable fees, patients might receive proper care and treatment at an early stage of the disease. A public meeting was held at

Criminals

Middle

class

* "Life and Work," etc., vol. ii., p. 229.
† Hansard, Third Series, cxix. 1237.

Freemasons' Hall to discuss the subject, and he made a speech from the chair of so exhaustive and stirring a nature that one of the audience, Mr. Thomas Holloway, a man of great wealth and generosity, was so deeply impressed with it that he determined on the spot to establish an institution on the lines laid down that day.   He was true, and more than true, to his word, and in 1885 the Prince of Wales opened the Holloway Sanitorium at Virginia Water, upon which up to that date Mr. Holloway had expended the sum of £300,000!

In 1877, owing to a fear, current in many minds, that patients were placed in asylums too easily, while the task of obtaining their discharge was too difficult, a Select Committee was appointed to inquire into the operation of the Lunacy Laws, so far as regarded the security afforded by them against violation of personal liberty.   Lord Shaftesbury was, naturally, the chief one to give evidence, and it was so conclusive that the Committee eventually reported that, " although the present system was not free from risks, which might be lessened, though not wholly removed by amendments in the existing law and practice, yet, assuming that the strongest cases against the present system were brought before them, allegations of *mala fides* or of serious abuses were not substantiated."

In commenting on Lord Shaftesbury's evidence, the *Journal of Mental Science* said : " We must heartily congratulate his lordship on the way in which the Act of 1845, his own handiwork, has passed through this examination. His lordship spoke with such a thorough mastery of every lunacy question about which he was asked, that his replies are the admiration of all his younger fellow-countrymen who are in any way interested in the welfare of the insane."

From 1828, when he first launched himself into the difficult question of the treatment of lunatics, to the end of his long career, Lord Shaftesbury kept himself *en rapport* with this subject; "painful, harassing, perplexing," he often found it to be, and depressing to the last degree to one of his sensitive and nervous temperament. But wherever his sympathies were excited his active labour invariably followed. And his sympathies were ever with the insane. One day he wrote in his diary: "I am visiting in authority to-day. I may be visited by authority to-morrow. God be praised that there are any visitations at all : time was when such visitations were unknown. What an awful condition that of a lunatic! His words are generally disbelieved, and his most innocent peculiarities perverted : it is natural it should be so ; we know him to be insane—at least, we are told that he is so—and we place ourselves on our guard— that is, we give to every word, look, gesture, a value and meaning which sometimes it cannot bear, and which it never would bear in ordinary life."

It was not till after seventeen years of labour and anxiety that he obtained the Lunacy Bill of 1845, and five years more were needed to carry it into operation. Then he was able to say, " It has effected, I know, prodigious relief, has forced the construction of many public asylums, and greatly multiplied inspection and care."

Later on he wrote: "Half a century has been devoted to this cause of the lunatics ; and through the wonderful mercy and power of God, the state now, as compared with the state *then*, would baffle, if description were attempted, any voice and any pen that were ever employed in spoken or written eloquence. *Non nobis, Domine.*"

It has been well said that if Lord Shaftesbury's labours on behalf of lunatics had been the sole work of his life it would have entitled him to a foremost rank among British philanthropists and social reformers.

CHAPTER IV.

CHIMNEY SWEEPERS AND CLIMBING BOYS.

THE Session of 1840 was signalised by Lord Ashley's exertions in furthering a Bill for the Regulation of Chimney Sweepers and Chimneys ; and it may be of interest to recall the main features of the struggle which ultimately led to the prohibition of the employment of climbing boys, as perhaps few things illustrate more accurately the slow and gradual manner in which humanity advanced in the old days, or the rapid progress which it has made during the present sixty years' reign.

In August 1760 there appeared in the *Public Advertiser* the following anonymous letter :—

"TO THE MAGISTRATES OF THE CITIES OF LONDON AND WESTMINSTER.

"GENTLEMEN,—There is in this capital an evil of a most crying nature, and which in my humble opinion is truly deserving of your attention. What I allude to is the number of chimney sweepers' boys that are to be met with in all parts of the town without either shoe or stocking to their feet. It is to be concluded that when their masters took them from their respective parishes they, in some form or other, bound themselves to provide them with some kind of clothing to defend them against the inclemency of the weather. If, therefore, you, gentlemen, would give directions to the proper officers that whenever they found a boy without proper covering for his nakedness they should inquire of him his master's name and place of abode, and summon him before you, in order that he might receive a punishment adequate to such an offence, you would soon put an end to it, and at the same time do an act which should reflect honour on yourselves.

> " I am, Gentlemen,
>> " Your very obedient servant,
>>> " AMBULATOR.

" *August* 1760."

This letter was read by good Jonas Hanway, the "Shaftesbury" of the eighteenth century, the originator of the Marine Society, the founder of the Magdalen Hospital and the world-known Foundling Hospital, the saviour of pauper children, the author of Hanway's Act of Parliament—" The Act for Keeping Poor Children Alive "—and the first man who ever used an umbrella !

No sooner had Jonas Hanway read the letter than he proceeded to make inquiries ; and he found that the only existing law enabled the master to gain parish apprentices at the very earliest age, but made no proper provision for their treatment ; that they were subject to the most cruel hardships ; that the mortality amongst them was fearful ; that they were liable to special and horrible complaints consequent upon the nature of their work, and that their morals and education were altogether neglected.

In 1785 Hanway published the result of his inquiries in a book entitled "A Sentimental History of Chimney Sweepers in London and Westminster, Showing the Necessity of Putting them under Regulation to Prevent the Grossest Inhumanity to the Climbing Boys, etc." In it he exposed the evils of the existing system, and showed, among other things, how orphan and illegitimate children were sold to the masters for 20s. or 30s. apiece, "being a smaller sum than the value of a *terrier*"; how they were forced up the chimneys in a perfectly naked state, and sometimes wild with terror ; how some were specially employed to ascend chimneys that were on fire, to the great danger of life and limb ; how they were let out for hire to other chimney sweepers, and in "off hours" were required to "call the streets"; how in some cases he had found that young girls were employed in the hateful climbing business ; and how this constant contact with soot produced rapid mortality from "sooty cancer," lung trouble, and skin diseases of a most irritating nature.

He pleaded for a climbing dress, as worn in France, Germany, and other countries; for a curtailment of the term of apprenticeship from seven to five years ; for magisterial inquiry and inspection ; for public baths, to free them, at least occasionally, from their garment of soot; and he pleaded earnestly in the name of humanity, on the ground of religion, liberty, and national character, and in the name of Christ, who "loved little children."

Hanway was even bold enough to hint that climbing boys might be dispensed with altogether, and instanced the practice in Scotland.

"The chimney sweepers in Edinburgh," he wrote, "are a part of the police of the city under the control of the magistrates. The number is fixed, and they are obliged every quarter to pay a certain sum for the benefit of such of their community as may be sick or in want. They have a house of call built at the expense of the city and in the centre of it, adjoining the town guard. Two of them watch every night in the guard room to be ready in case of fire. They are all fire*men*, and expert in extinguishing flames. The soot they collect is sold for the common benefit of the whole fraternity. No boys are employed. When any chimney is required to be swept two of these sweepers attend with a birch besom similar to that used by our oastlers, a short ladder, and a rope. One of them goes out at the garret window, and, securing the ladder, mounts to the top of the chimney, whence the besom is let down, and with the assistance of his companion below, very regularly sweep clean every side of the chimney, in which they are very expert."

Referring to the number of crippled, bandy-legged, and otherwise distorted climbing boys to be seen any day in the streets, he says that "beginning to climb before the knee-bone has acquired a solidity, the daily pressure necessarily gives the leg a twist, if it does not distort the ankles." He described the condition of one boy, twelve years of age, a permanent cripple on crutches, hardly three feet seven inches in stature, who began to climb before he was five years old, his bones not having acquired a fit degree of strength. ("The same treatment of the colt," he says, "would be deemed a transgression against all the rules of rustic economy towards the beasts that perish.") "His legs and feet resemble an S more than an L. His hair felt like hog's bristles. He was blind for six months, but still did his work. He still sweeps chimneys, using his crippled knees uncovered and unfortified."

Waxing warm with his subject, he charged the magistrates of the country with being accessories to murder : " If we rob a boy of his limbs or his sight, what compensation do we make him ? We make him none, but sit down calmly to the repast dressed by the fire of the chimney where the boy, perhaps, was offered as a victim to a *cruel custom* ! "

"Let any one examine into the merits of the cause," he says at the conclusion of his book. "With all the laborious efforts which these boys make for a support, their bruised bodies, weakened eyes, frequent wounds, lungs stuffed, unwashen, unclothed, uncomfortable lodging and scanty diet irregularly supplied, indeed constitute 'A Sentimental History,' equal to any of the miseries which human nature seems capable of supporting ; and how this could be connived at in any country professing the lowest degree of civilisation, whatever religion it might be of, would be truly wonderful; but in a country professing Christianity in its utmost purity, and liberty in its most uncorrupted state, is yet more wonderful; and if the evil is suffered to remain any longer it must level us with nations whom we call barbarians, if it does not ultimately draw on us the vengeance of Heaven. The magistrate and the legislator, clergy and laity, sovereign and subject, all in their respective stations are called upon, as it were by a voice from heaven, to succour these poor children."

Alas! the "evil was suffered to remain," with only slight modifications from time to time, for over a hundred years, to the everlasting shame of our country.

One result of Jonas Hanway's efforts was that in 1788 an Act was passed forbidding master sweepers to have more than six apprentices or to take them under eight years of age.

At the beginning of the present century one or two societies were formed for bettering the condition of climbing boys, and in 1817 Parliament referred the question to a Select Committee, whose report was "a record of sickening horrors." An "Amending Bill" was passed in the House of Commons, but was thrown out by the House of Lords, and matters remained *in statu quo*.

A number of public-spirited individuals then joined in offering considerable premiums to any one who would invent a method of cleaning chimneys by mechanical means, so as to supersede the necessity of climbing boys. Various inventions were in consequence produced, and, to encourage the masters to use them, machines were presented to them gratuitously. They were all more or less after the style of the one now in general use, consisting, as every one knows, of a brush and some hollow tubes, which fasten into each other by means of brass sockets.

It was not until 1834 that the introduction of the sweeping machine made any material alteration in the custom of sending young boys up the chimneys at the peril, and not seldom, even at that date, at the sacrifice of their lives. In that year an Act was passed, prohibiting the employment of any apprentice under ten years of age; making it a misdemeanour to send him up a chimney on fire for the purpose of extinguishing it; imposing penalties for the ill-treatment of apprentices, and enacting that flues should not in future measure less than fourteen inches by nine, and that all projecting angles should be rounded off! Public opinion was too weak to demand that climbers should be dispensed with altogether; masters, builders, owners of property, and insurance companies were too strong to submit to any drastic legislation as to a new construction of chimneys to render this possible. Rectangular flues were still very common, and while they were so it was absolutely necessary—so it was argued—that they should be swept by hand.

In the year 1840 a Bill was brought forward in the House of Commons for " the Regulation of Chimney Sweepers and Chimneys "; and Lord Ashley, although his hands were full of other legislation, threw his whole heart and soul into the subject. He had read the work of Jonas Hanway, and had long felt that something ought to be done. Now, the matter being pressed upon his consideration, he went into it with that thoroughness which characterised all his efforts.

If, at any period of his career, he had taken the advice of his friend Robert Southey, to abstain from making himself an eye-witness of the horrors he was striving to abate—warning him at the same time that the distressful recollections would be *burnt in* upon his soul to the injury of his health and mental activity—he would, by accepting that advice, have cut away a very large proportion of his usefulness. The warning was kindly given, for these horrible sights *did* burn themselves into his brain, and the constant surroundings of suffering and despair, new and old, did make him a sad and melancholy man. But for the joy that was set before him—the joy of seeing homes made happier and young lives redeemed from cruel and unnatural toil—he endured throughout his long life that which was repugnant to his refined and sensitive nature, and persistently continued to be "an eye-witness of the horrors he was striving to abate."

It was so in the matter of the climbing boys: he went to see them at their work and in their so-called "homes"; he visited their masters, put himself into direct communication with the hard-hearted employers on the one hand and the generous philanthropists opposed to them on the other, and he collected such a mass of information that he fairly made the House of Commons aghast when he narrated how, notwithstanding previous attempts to alleviate their wrongs, these infant chimney sweeps were still being driven naked up the foul flues, where they were exposed to be scorched, roasted alive, or stifled, and from whence they often came down with bruised and excoriated bodies, to pass the hours of rest naked on the soot heaps, and contract tormenting skin disease from the villainous stuff.*

Notwithstanding a strong opposition in the House of Lords—the halting-place of so many beneficent movements—and a formidable attempt to shelve it by referring it to a Select Committee, the Bill was carried successfully, and passed into law in August 1840. By this Act † the compelling or allowing a person under twenty-one years of age to ascend or descend a chimney, or to enter a flue for the purpose of sweeping or cleaning it, or of extinguishing fire, was prohibited, under a penalty of not more than £10 or less than £5. It was further provided by the same Act that no child under sixteen years of age should be apprenticed to a chimney sweeper, and it contained regulations as to the future construction of chimneys.

Immediately after the passage of the Bill Lord Ashley used his utmost efforts to secure obedience to it, and in some cases he even brought test actions

---

* Hansard, Third Series, lv. 108.
† 3 & 4 Vic., cap. 85.

against persons who infringed the law. A characteristic entry in his diary refers to two of such suits:—

"*August 24th.* Succeeded in both my suits. I undertook them in a spirit of justice. I constituted myself, no doubt, a defender of the poor, to see that the poor and miserable had their rights; but 'I looked, and there was none to help; I wondered that there was none to uphold: therefore God's arm, it brought salvation unto me; and His fury, it upheld me!' I stood to lose several hundred pounds, but I have not lost a farthing; I have advanced the cause, done individual justice, anticipated many calamities by this forced prevention, and soothed, I hope, many angry, discontented Chartist spirits by showing them that men of rank and property can, and do, care for the rights and feelings of all their brethren. Let no one ever despair of a good cause for want of coadjutors; let him persevere, persevere, persevere, and God will raise him up friends and assistants!"*

It was hoped, and by many believed, that this long-suffered abuse was now dead. But abuses die hard, and for more than thirty years after the Bill of 1840 became law, little children, from four to eight years of age, the majority of them orphans, the rest bartered or sold by brutal parents, were trained to force their way up the long, narrow, winding passages of chimneys to clear away the soot. We cannot follow the movement through all its stages, but must content ourselves

* "Life and Work," vol. i., p. 301.

by glancing at a few of the direct efforts to crush the evil.

In June 1851, the month when Lord Shaftesbury took his seat in the House of Lords—the "Statue Gallery," the "Dormitory," the "Nova Zembla," as he variously called it—he "broke cover in a bit of humanity-mongering about chimney sweepers"; but although his speech was successful, it did not lead to decisive action. In the following year, therefore, he renewed his efforts on their behalf by giving his support to a Bill for their relief. He "suffered actual tortures through solicitude for prevention of these horrid cruelties," he feared the "accursed system was returning to London," he was mystified that efforts for their real relief had been so long unavailing ; and when the Government in the House of Commons threw out the Bill, and said not a word of sympathy for the wretched children, nor of desire to amend the law, he wrote on the Sunday following : "Very sad and low about the loss of the Sweeps Bill—the prolonged sufferings, the terrible degradation, the licensed tyranny, the helpless subjection, the enormous mass of cruelty and crime on the part of parents and employers are overwhelming."

Again, in 1855 he was busy with a Bill for further legislation on behalf of chimney sweeps, but, owing chiefly to the active resistance of Sir G. Grey, he was compelled to withdraw it. Then came a long pause, and it was not until 1861, when the Children's Employment Commission was appointed, and climbing boys were included in the scope of the inquiry, that the matter was again before the country. Lord Shaftesbury eagerly watched the evidence, carefully read the Blue Books, found that he had by no means overstated the case in his previous utterances, and in 1863-4 brought the whole matter before the House of Lords, with the result that he actually succeeded in carrying a Bill which made it unlawful for a chimney sweeper to take into a house with him any assistant under sixteen years of age, and which empowered magistrates, in case of a breach of the law, " to impose imprisonment with hard labour instead of a fine." But even this measure did not terminate the prevalent abuses. Two years later, in their Fifth Report, the Children's Employment Commission gave evidence showing clearly that the Act of 1864 had failed to answer its intended purpose.

Ever on the alert and ever ready to press into his cause any circumstance that could forward measures in which he was interested, there came to Lord Shaftesbury's notice in 1872 an account of a climbing boy who had been suffocated in a flue in Staffordshire. This gave him an opportunity of appealing to the public in the columns of the *Times*, and of drawing attention to the case in the House of Lords; but nothing came of it. In the following year he drew attention to the case of " a poor little chimney sweeper, seven-and-a-half years old, killed in a flue at Washington, in the county of Durham," again without any success.

But in 1875 he called the attention of the Government to the case of one George Brewster, a boy of fourteen, who had been suffocated in a flue at Cambridge. At last the public mind was excited; George Brewster's master was sentenced to six months' hard labour. The *Times*, in commenting on this ridiculously light sentence, said boldly, in a vigorous article, that "whoever deliberately authorised and permitted the employment of this unfortunate boy are morally guilty of the crime of murder," and expressed the opinion that "the time has come for a final review of the system"* under which such things were possible.

Lord Shaftesbury was not slow to take the hint, and on April 20th, 1875, he gave notice of a Bill on the subject. "One hundred and two years have elapsed," he wrote, "since the good Jonas Hanway brought the brutal iniquity before the public, yet in many parts of England and Ireland it still prevails, with the full knowledge and consent of thousands of all classes."

The country was stirred; the *Times* "assisted generously"; on the platform, in the Legislature, and in the press Lord Shaftesbury worked persistently; and, in that same session, the fetters of the poor climbing slaves were broken, and there was rolled away, for ever, "one of the greatest reproaches to the civilisation of this country."

Years afterwards, at a great public meeting, a speaker, as speakers very often did if they had anything to say about the poor, mentioned the name of Lord Shaftesbury. Instantly there was loud clapping. "And what do you know about Lord Shaftesbury?"

* *Times*, March 25th, 1875.

asked the speaker of the people before him. "Know of him?" answered a man, rising up among the crowd. "Why, sir, I'm a chimbley sweeper, and what did he do for me? Didn't he pass the Bill? Why, when I was a little 'un, sir, I had to go up chimbleys, and many a time I've come down with bleedin' feet and knees and a'most chokin'. And he passed the Bill and saved us from all that. *That's* what I know, sir, of Lord Shaftesbury!"

CHAPTER V.

CHILDREN IN MINES AND COLLIERIES.

SO soon as Lord Ashley stood out in the world's eyes as the champion of the oppressed factory hands and the ill-used climbing boys, every other suffering class began to look upon him as the Hercules who was to cleanse the Augean Stable of its accumulated mass of pollution, and piteously invoked his aid. There was no need for this: already his heart was full of sympathy, as his head was full of schemes, for their relief; and no sooner had he seen the factory children and climbing boys safe in harbour than he turned his attention to the case of the thousands of children who stood outside the protection of the Acts he had succeeded in carrying. For a long time this subject had been on his mind, and, in reply to certain taunts that had been levelled at him to the effect that he had given narrow and exclusive attention to one class alone, to the prejudice of others equally oppressed and not less numerous, he moved, on August 4th, 1840, for "a Commission of Inquiry into the employment of the children of the poorer classes in mines and collieries, and in the various branches of trade and manufacture in which numbers of children worked together, not being included in the provisions of the Act for regulating the employment of children and young persons in mills and factories; and to collect information as to the ages at which they are employed, the number of hours they are engaged in work, the time allowed each day for meals, and as to the actual state, condition, and treatment of such children, and as to the effects of such employment, both with regard to their morals and their bodily health."

The children he had in his mind's eye were principally those who were employed in irksome and unhealthy work, such as earthenware, porcelain, hosiery, pin-making, needle-making, manufacture of arms, nail-making, card-setting, draw-boy-weaving, ironwork, forges, etc.; iron foundries, glass trade, collieries, calico-printing, tobacco manufacture, button factories, bleaching and paper mills.

In this new crusade Lord Ashley again addressed himself to the interests of children, on the ground that the future hopes of a country must be laid in the character and condition of its children, and that, however right it may be to attempt, it is almost fruitless to expect, the reformation of its adults. To ensure a vigorous and moral manhood the only effectual course was to train them aright from their earliest years, and so reserve the full development of their moral and physical energies for the services hereafter of our common country.

He brought some serious indictments against each of the several departments of industry he had named,

especially as regarded mines and collieries and calico-
print works ; and cited upon high authority so many
cases of gross cruelty and injustice that he fairly
startled the House. Anticipating the question as to
what remedy for these evils he could suggest, he frankly
replied that he was not prepared to suggest any—he
could only state the case and explain his motives.
The first of these was to place, if possible, all children
in the land in such a position and under such circumstances as to lay them open to an aggressive movement
for education ; to reserve and cherish their physical
energies ; to cultivate and improve their moral part ;
both of which, taken separately or conjointly, are
essential to the peace, security, and progress of the
empire. His further motive was a desire to remove
those spectacles of suffering and oppression from the
eyes of the poorer classes, spectacles that perplexed
the peaceable and exasperated the discontented, that
tended to render capital odious, as wealth was known
to them only by its oppressions. "They judge of it,"
he said, " by what they see immediately around them ;
they know but little beyond their own narrow sphere ;
they do not extend their view over the whole surface
of the land, and so perceive and understand the compensating advantages that wealth and property bestow
on the community at large. With so much ignorance
on one side, and so much oppression on the other, I
have never wondered that perilous errors and bitter
hatreds have prevailed ; but I have wondered much
and been very thankful that they have prevailed so
little."

" Only let us exhibit those evils," he said in conclusion, "there is wit enough, experience enough,
activity enough, and principle enough in the country
to devise some remedy. For my own part I will say,
though possibly I may be charged with cant and
hypocrisy, that I have been bold enough to undertake
this task because I must regard the objects of it as
being created, as ourselves, by the same Maker, redeemed by the same Saviour, and destined to the
same immortality."

To his great surprise—for he had entertained
grave doubts as to how this wide subject would be
received—the motion was agreed to after only a
very brief discussion, and the much desired Commission granted! "The behaviour of the Government
towards me was most kind and gentlemanlike!"
he said.

It was not till May in 1842 that the Report of the
Commissioners * was issued, and it contained such
startling revelations of cruelty, misery, and depravity
that, despite the efforts of the Home Office to hold it
back, and of the Secretary of State to prevent its
sale, it obtained a publicity very seldom accorded to
Blue Books. Public indignation and excitement were
aroused to an extraordinary pitch; and, taking advantage of this, Lord Ashley moved on June 7th for
leave to bring in a Bill to make regulations respecting
the age and sex of children and young persons
employed in the mines and collieries of the United
Kingdom.

* Parliamentary Papers, 1842, xv., xvi., xvii.

Taking for his text-book the Report of the Commissioners, he wove together and delivered with great force a statement of facts that was simply appalling. It was found that in Northumberland and Durham there were nearly as many women and children as men in the pits, and in Lancashire and Yorkshire a much larger ratio, while in many other places the same system prevailed—in the east of Scotland almost universally. In Ireland, however, to her honour be it said, neither children of tender years nor females of any age were employed in underground operations. In many of these mines and collieries the children began work at the age of five or six years, others at seven or eight. We have told of the terror experienced by little boy-climbers in their first introduction to dark and narrow flues reeking with soot; and not less horrible was the child's employment in the damp, dark, and close mine.

Take one example. "The first employment of a very young child was that of a 'trapper,' and any occupation more barbarous it is difficult to conceive. The ventilation of a mine was a very complicated affair, and cannot easily be explained in a few words. Suffice it to say that, were a door, or trap, left open after the passage of a coal carriage through it, the consequences would be very serious, causing great heat and closeness where the miners were at work, and perchance an explosion. Behind each door, therefore, a little child, or trapper, was seated, whose duty it was, on hearing the approach of a whirley, or coal-carriage, to pull open the door and shut it again immediately the whirley had passed. From the time the first coal was brought forward in the morning, until the last whirley had passed at night—that is to say, for twelve or fourteen hours a day—the trapper was at his monotonous, deadening work. He had to sit alone in the pitchy darkness and the horrible silence, exposed to damp, and unable to stir for more than a dozen paces with safety, lest he should be found neglecting his duty and suffer accordingly. He dared not go to sleep—the punishment was the 'strap,' applied with brutal severity. Many of the mines were infested with rats, mice, beetles, and other vermin ; and stories are told of rats so bold that they would eat the horses' food in the presence of the miners, and have been known to run off with the lighted candles in their mouths and explode the gas. All the circumstances of a little trapper's life were full of horror, and upon nervous, sensitive children the effect was terrible, producing a state of imbecility approaching almost to idiocy. Except on Sunday they never saw the sun ; they had no hours of relaxation, their meals were mostly eaten in the dark, and their 'homes' were with parents who devoted them to this kind of life." *

Many of the pits were so wet that the people had to work all day over their shoes in water, at the same time that water was dripping constantly from the roof. In other pits, instead of dripping, it constantly "rained," as they called it, so that in a short time

* " Life and Work," etc., vol. i., pp. 413-14.

after they commenced the labour of the day their clothes were drenched ; and in that state, with their feet in water, they worked all day, and at night had in many cases to walk a mile or two to their homes without changing their clothes.

In some of the collieries the main roadways did not exceed a yard in height ; in others they varied from 22 to 28 inches, so that in such places the youngest children could only work in the most constrained position. The ways were so low that only little boys could work in them, which they did naked, and often in mud and water, drawing sledge tubs by the girdle and chain. The girdle was bound round the waist of the child, to which was attached a chain which passed under the legs and was attached to the cart. The child was obliged to work on all fours, and the chain passed under what in that posture might be called the hind-legs ; and thus, with blisters on their sides caused by the girdle, and terrible chafings of the legs from the chains, they crawled for weary hours through avenues not so good as a common sewer, quite as wet and oftentimes more contracted, and in a temperature described as perfectly intolerable. "I went into the pit at seven years of age," said Robert North, in his evidence before the Commissioners. "When I drew by the girdle and chain the skin was broken, and the blood ran down. . . . If we said anything they would beat us. I have seen many draw at six. They must do it or be beat. They cannot straighten their backs during the day. I have sometimes pulled till my hips have hurt me so that I have not known what to do with myself."

Incredible as it may seem in this day, girls were employed as trappers and "hurriers" in common with boys. "The girls," said Lord Ashley, "are of all ages from seven to twenty-one. They commonly work quite naked down to the waist, and are dressed— so far as they are dressed at all—in a loose pair of trousers. These are seldom whole on either sex. In many of the collieries the adult colliers, whom these girls serve, work perfectly naked. . . . Any sight more disgustingly indecent or revolting than these girls at work can scarcely be imagined."

In this condition they had to drag heavy weights, some 12,000, some 14,000, some 16,000 yards daily.

"Coal-bearing" was an equally cruel slavery, and was almost always performed by women and children. "They carry coal on their backs," said one of the Commissioners, "on unrailed roads, with burdens varying from ¾ cwt. to 3 cwts., a cruelty revolting to humanity. I found a little girl only six years old," he added, "carrying ½ cwt., and making regularly fourteen long journeys a day. With a burden varying from 1 cwt. to 1½ cwt., the height ascended and the distance along the roads added together exceeded in each journey the height of St. Paul's Cathedral. And it not unfrequently happens that the tugs break, and the load falls on those females who are following, who are of course struck off the ladders into the depths below." No wonder that one poor girl should say,

"We are worse off than horses: they draw on iron rails, and we on flat floors."

The hours of labour were everywhere excessive, varying from eleven to sixteen out of the twenty-four, while in the great majority of the mines night-work was a part of the ordinary system of labour. "I have repeatedly wrought the twenty-four hours," said Anne Hamilton, a girl of seventeen, "and after two hours of rest and my peas (soup) have returned to the pit and worked another twelve hours."

The physical effects of this system were stunted growth, crippled gait, irritation of head, back, and feet, diseases of the spine and of the heart and lungs. The most destructive and frequent diseases were asthma and rheumatism. In addition to these evils, there were those resulting from the violence of the brutal overseers and their assistants. Let the words of a few witnesses, who gave evidence before the Commissioners, tell their own tale :—

"I was bullied by a man to do what was beyond my strength," said Isaac Tipstone. "I would not because I could not. The man threw me down and kicked out two of my ribs."

"My boy," said Hannah Neale, "ten years old, was at work; about half a year since his toe was cut off by the bind falling. Notwithstanding this the loader made him work until the end of the day, although he was in the greatest pain."

"A man," said Hannah Craven, aged eleven, "flung a piece of coal as big as my head at me, and it struck me in the back."

" I remember meeting," said the Sub-Commissioner, " one of the boys crying very bitterly, and bleeding from a wound in his cheek. I found his master, who told me, in a tone of savage defiance, that the child was one of the slow ones, who would only move when he saw blood, and that by throwing a piece of coal at him he had accomplished his purpose, and that he often adopted the like means." *

We have purposely given only a very few examples of the evils that Lord Ashley was seeking to abate, and those of a mild type, for others are too sickening to record in detail.

In the course of his speech he said : " Only a few days ago I went over the new prison at Pentonville. Never have I seen such preparations as are there made for securing a proper degree of comfort to the prisoner—such care for light, such care for ventilation, such care that every necessary requirement of the

* " One curious error was made in the debates on this Report of the Commission. It was stated that a miner had thrown a hundredweight at a boy, and hurt him seriously. The statement made some sensation, but admitted of a very simple explanation. The miners, an uneducated race, kept all their records in the mine by tallies or, as they called them, cuts. A cut was a piece of wood on which notches for reckoning were made. It was given in evidence that a miner had thrown a cut at a boy and hurt him seriously. The clerk who copied out the evidence had never heard of a cut, and, changing one letter, wrote ' cwt.' The printer, improving on the error, gave the word at full— ' hundredweight.' We ourselves had the curiosity some years ago to search out the mistake in the very voluminous evidence attached to the Commissioners' report."—*Edinburgh Review*, April 1887, p. 367.

prisoner should be furnished.   He is to have books, tools, instruction—to hear the human voice at least fourteen times a day.   Sir, I find no fault with that ; but I pray you to bear in mind that all this is done for persons who have forfeited their liberty by the laws of their country ; but here you have a number of poor children, whose only crime is that they are poor, and who are sent down to these horrid dens, subjected to every privation and every variety of brutal treatment, and on whom you inflict even a worse curse than this—the curse of dark and perpetual ignorance."   And he was at a white heat of righteous indignation when in a loud voice he cried to the House to "undo the heavy burthens and let the oppressed go free ! "

The cry was not in vain.   For "two and a half hours the House listened so attentively that you might have heard a pin drop, broken only by loud and 'repeated marks of approbation."   Many strong men wept during its delivery.   Richard Cobden, who had been his opponent on the Factory Question, came over to him and said, " I don't think I have ever been put into such a frame of mind in the whole course of my life as I have been by your speech," and from that day friendship sprang up between them.   The Prince Consort read " every syllable of the speech to the Queen," and both expressed their profound sympathy in the " arduous, but glorious task."

The Bill passed into law in a single session, in spite of the coldness of the Government, the peers, and even of the Church.   It was a splendid victory, and an inestimable blessing to the country.   We can but briefly summarise what the provisions of the Act* were :—From the time of passing the Act no female, other than such as were employed previously, was to work in any mine or colliery ; and that after three months from that date no female under eighteen years old should be so employed ; *nor any female whatever* after March 1st, 1843.   After this date also no males were to be employed under ten years of age.   No person to be apprenticed under ten years of age, nor for longer than eight years (except in the case of engine-wrights and others who were very occasionally at work underground).   When there were vertical or other shafts, no steam or other engine to be entrusted to the care of a person under the age of fifteen ; in the case of a windlass or gin worked by a horse or other animal, the driver to be considered the person in charge.   After three months from the passing of the Act proprietors of mines or collieries were not to pay workmen their wages at any tavern or public-house.   Stringent arrangements were made to enforce these regulations ; Inspectors, appointed by the Secretary of State for the Home Department, were empowered to enter and examine all works in mines and collieries, and to report concerning them to the Government, and heavy fines were to be inflicted upon offenders against any of the provisions of the Act.

* 5 & 6 Vic., cap. 99.

Of course, as in all sweeping reforms, there was trouble at first, consequent upon so many young persons being thrown for a time out of employment ; but this was a temporary difficulty, and altogether insignificant in comparison with the hateful system that will ever be remembered as a great blot on the humanity and civilisation of this country.

CHAPTER VI.

IT will be remembered that when the Children's Employment Commission gave in their first report, attention was called to a large number of trades and branches of labour outside the scope of the Factory Acts. The most glaring abuses revealed in that Report related to the employment of women and children in mines and colleries, and that subject, as we have seen, Lord Ashley attacked forthwith.

When the Second Report of the Commissioners was presented, the subject of greatest importance, as it seemed to him, to be dealt with was the question of the employment of children in calico-print works; and on February 18th, 1845, he brought forward a Bill to regulate their employment in that trade.

These repeated attacks on child-labour naturally gave rise to the impression that the representative of the factory operatives was engaged in a gigantic crusade against the employers of labour generally, and, as naturally, the latter rallied in defence of their order. Every step taken in any direction was met by the formidable opposition of masters, who feared that "the hope of their gains was gone." Fears were expressed that trade would be ruined, that pauperism must necessarily increase largely, that vested interests were being unwarrantably interfered with. What was more lamentable than anything else was the fact that so many of the parents of the children whose social elevation was aimed at, were opposed to protective measures ; so great was their moral degradation that they did not want their children to be educated, and were willing, without hesitation, to sacrifice their future welfare through life for the immediate advantage or gratification obtained by the pittance derived from the child's earnings.

But whenever Lord Ashley had a cause at heart— and especially one affecting the welfare of little children—no amount of opposition could deter him from his purpose ; he would not—

> " bate a jot
> Of heart or hope, but still bear up and steer
> Right onward."

The matter to which he now addressed himself was a large one, affecting, at that time alone, the welfare of at least 25,000 persons.

Calico-printing, with its subsidiary processes of bleaching and dyeing, was carried on to the greatest extent in the cotton districts of Lancashire, Cheshire, Derbyshire, and the east of Scotland ; there were also a few print works near London, and several near Dublin. A large proportion of the children and young persons employed in this branch of trade were girls, the proportion in Lancashire being upwards of one-third of the whole number under thirteen. Children began work at as early an age as between four and five, and the great majority between eight and nine.

In making their investigations the Commissioners clearly pointed out that there was probably no description of manufacture in which the convenience and comfort of the places in which the various operations were carried on differed so materially in different establishments, and even in different departments of the same establishment, as in calico-printing With the view of lessening, as far as practicable, the noxiousness of these operations, some proprietors spared neither trouble nor expense to secure proper ventilation, temperature, and drainage ; but in a large number of cases these conditions of the place of work were deplorably neglected, and it was to these, of course, that Lord Ashley mainly directed his attention. Let one or two examples suffice.

The "hooking" and "lashing-out" rooms, and the "singeing" room were very disagreeable places, the air of which was filled with dust, and in the latter with small burnt particles, which exceedingly irritated the eyes, throat, and nostrils. The temperature of the workshops usually varied from 65° to 80°, while that to which the stenters were exposed was very high—from 85° to 100°, and sometimes 110° or fever heat. Of course this was very injurious to health, more especially as the steam, rising from wet goods hung up to dry, was more suffocating and oppressive than dry heat would have been. Many girls, and especially the stove girls, would often faint from exhaustion; while injured sight and throat diseases were the consequence of labour in other departments.

It was not, however, with the nature of the labour, which was not in itself heavy, that Lord Ashley was chiefly concerned, but with the continuity of doing it for so many hours, that produced so debilitating an effect on both mind and body.

The regular hours of work in the different departments of the print-field were rarely less than twelve, including the time allowed for meals; but it was by no means uncommon in all the districts for children from five to six years old to be kept at work for fourteen and even sixteen hours consecutively. As a matter of fact, there could scarcely be said to be any regular hours, for all the block-printers were in the habit of working overtime, and as they were paid by the piece, and were independent of machinery, they were at liberty to work what hours they pleased. One man told the Commissioners: "I began to work between eight and nine o'clock on Wednesday night, but the boy had been sweeping the shop from Wednesday morning. You will scarcely believe it, but it is true, I never left the shop till six o'clock on the Saturday morning, and I had never stopped working all that time. I was knocked up, and the boy was almost insensible." Instances were found of young girls working at the steam cans for thirty-eight hours in succession—a very exhausting labour—

and of little children under eight years of age working all night through for three or four nights a week. In the morning these poor children seemed as though they were suffering from the effects of gross intoxication ; their eyes were inflamed, their gait unsteady, their hands tremulous, their faces deadly pale or unnaturally flushed. A deputation of calico-printers admitted that "night-work was doubly distressing on this account : that as a great quantity of gas was burnt in rooms badly ventilated, the air was hurtful to breathe and bad for the constitution." It must, moreover, be borne in mind that the print works were always most busy during the winter, in preparation for the spring trade—a time of year when toil and exposure were the least endurable.

It was proved up to the hilt that with proper management all this excessive toil was unnecessary, and that night-work was an evil no less to the employer than to the employed. An influential firm favoured one of the Commissioners with an inspection of their books, which showed rates of production in their roller-printing machines during a period of four months, when they worked fifteen hours a day. "The proportion of *spoiled work*," he says, "from the beginning of the first to the end of the fourth month actually doubled itself, when the average production of the machines decreased from 100 to 90 per cent. In fact, the amount of spoiled work increased to such an alarming extent that the parties referred to felt themselves obliged to shorten the hours of labour to avoid loss, and as soon as the alteration was made the amount of spoiled work sank to its former level."

Between the periods of the first and second reading of the Bill, Sir James Graham, as Home Secretary, caused all the inspectors of factories to examine the Bill in the light of their own experience, and to attend to such objections as the master printers might urge against it. The result of these inquiries was to induce the Government to assent to the Bill in a modified form. Lord Ashley had proposed that its provisions should apply to bleach works, dye works, and calendering works, as well as to print works ; but Sir James would only agree to the last-named application. This was a great disappointment to Lord Ashley, but he accepted the Government offer as a means of securing the passing of a Bill which would at any rate be a movement in the wished-for direction, and which would not preclude further measures of a similar kind in subsequent sessions. After amendments in both Houses it passed into law as " The Print Works Act, 8 & 9 Vic., cap. 29," and came into force on January 1st, 1846.

Henceforth all calico-print works came under proper inspection ; no child could be employed under eight years of age, and no child under thirteen or young person under sixteen at night. A certain amount of schooling was prescribed for every child and young person, the schoolmaster to be controlled in certain matters by the inspectors.

It was not by any means the kind of Act Lord Ashley had wished it to be, but on the principle that "half a loaf is better than no bread" he accepted it, and subsequent experience showed that it mitigated to a very large extent the evils that had once existed, and greatly ameliorated the condition of the young workers.

It was anticipated by many that Lord Ashley would immediately proceed to deal with other trades and manufactures, but his hands were too full with other burning questions, and he did not consider that either the time was ripe or his influence sufficient to carry any further measures of the kind to a successful issue. "The House is weary of these narratives of suffering and shame," he said; "the novelty is past, and the difficulty, the apparent difficulty, of a remedy remains; it catches, therefore, at any excuse for inattention, and damns the advocate for the toiling thousands by courteous indifference."

It would be wide of our present purpose to record here, even in the briefest outline, the remedial measures that were passed to benefit children and young persons in all the various departments of trade, as an outcome of the inquiries of the Children's Employment Commission. There was one class, however, viz., children employed in brickfields, who, by a technical difficulty, were excluded from the protection of these measures, while those employed in pottery and porcelain works were included. It was an anomaly and an injustice which Lord Shaftesbury determined he would set right; but it was not until the year 1871 that he was able to do so.

Meanwhile there had been many workers on behalf

of the brickfield children, the chief of whom was George Smith, of Coalville. He had been to the manner born, and a passage from his own experience will better illustrate the case than any other evidence that could be selected :—

"When a child of about seven years of age" (that is to say in the year 1838) "I was employed by a relative to assist him in making bricks. It is not my wish to say anything against him ; but, like most of his class at that time, and like many even now (1871), he thought kicks and blows formed the best means of obtaining the maximum of work from a lad ; and, as if these were not enough, excessively long hours of work were added.

"At nine years of age my employment consisted in continually carrying about 40 lb. of clay upon my head from the clay heap to the table on which the bricks were made. When there was no clay I had to carry the same weight of bricks. This labour had to be performed, almost without intermission, for thirteen hours daily. Sometimes my labours were increased by my having to work all night at the kilns.

"The result of the prolonged and severe labour to which I was subjected, combined with the cruel treatment experienced by me at the hands of the adult labourers, are shown in marks that are borne by me to this day. On one occasion I had to perform a very heavy amount of labour. After my customary day's work I had to carry 1200 nine-inch bricks from the maker to the floors on which they are placed to harden. The total distance thus walked by me that night was not less than fourteen miles, seven miles of which I traversed with 11 lb. weight of clay in my arms, besides lifting the unmade clay and carrying it some distance to the maker. The total quantity of clay thus carried by me was $5\frac{1}{2}$ tons. For all this labour I received sixpence! The fatigue thus experienced brought on a serious illness, which for several weeks prevented me from resuming work." *

In 1863 George Smith, who had determined on his deliverance from the slavery of the brickfields to make the liberation of his fellows one of the great labours of his life, fell in with Mr. Robert Baker, one of Her Majesty's Inspectors of Factories, and with his aid ventilated the whole subject in public. By letters to the press and appeals to private individuals, by speeches and pamphlets, he kept the agitation alive.

One of these pamphlets was sent to Mr. Mundella, M.P., who wrote in acknowledgment of it, " I have determined to bring the matter before the House in some shape or other " ; and another to Lord Shaftesbury, who replied, " This state of things is simply wicked, and the continuance of it without excuse." In June 1871, public indignation having been strongly roused, Mr. Mundella introduced into the House of Commons a Bill—" The Factories Acts (Brick and

* " George Smith, of Coalville: The Story of an Enthusiast," by Edwin Hodder (Jas. Nisbet & Co., Ltd.), p. 26

Tile Yards) Extension Bill, 1871 "—and on July 11th
Lord Shaftesbury moved an Address to the Crown
in the House of Lords.

Although he was then seventy years of age, he had
not abandoned—nor did he till the end—his habit
of thoroughly sifting and personally inquiring into
and inspecting every phase of the subject with
which he had to deal ; and we think the following
extract from his speech in moving the Address,
giving the result of his personal observations, will be
regarded as inimitable :—

" I went down to a brickfield," he said, "and made
a considerable inspection. On approaching I first
saw, at a distance, what appeared like eight or ten
pillars of clay, which, I thought, were placed there in
order to indicate how deep the clay had been worked.
On walking up I found to my astonishment that these
pillars were living beings. They were so like the
ground on which they stood, their features were so
indistinguishable, their dress so besoiled and covered
with clay, their flesh so like their dress, that, until
I approached and saw them move, I believed them
to be products of the earth. When I approached
they were so scared at seeing anything not like
themselves, that they ran away screaming, as though
something Satanic was approaching. I followed them
to their work, and then I saw what Elihu Burritt has
so well described. I saw little children, three parts
naked, tottering under the weight of wet clay—some
of it on their heads and some on their shoulders—

and little girls, with huge masses of wet, cold, and dripping clay pressed on their abdomens. Moreover, the unhappy children were exposed to the most sudden transitions of heat and cold ; for after carrying their burdens of wet clay, they had to endure the heat of the kiln, and to enter places where the heat was so fierce that I was not myself able to remain more than two or three minutes. Can it be denied that in these brickfields men, women, and children, especially poor female children, are brought down to a point of degradation and suffering lower than the beasts of the field ? No man with a sense of humanity, or with the aspirations of a Christian, could go through these places and not feel that what he saw was a disgrace to the country and ought not for a moment to be allowed to continue."

Next day he wrote to Mr. George Smith : " Thank God I carried the Address last night. We shall have this year a Bill for the children in the brickyards. Bless God for His grace on your efforts."

And so it was. Everything was got through in that same session, and on January 1st, 1872, thousands of little white slaves were set free by the coming into force of the famous clause that declared that " no female under the age of sixteen years, and no child under the age of ten years, shall be employed in the manufacture of bricks and tiles, not being ornamental tiles ; and any female or child who is employed in contravention of this section shall be deemed to be employed in a manner contrary to the provisions of the Factory Acts 1833 to 1871 and the Workshops Acts 1867 to 1871."

For thirty-four years Lord Shaftesbury had been exposing the evils which beset children, young persons, and women in the manufacturing industries, and measure after measure had been carried for their relief: inhuman hours of toil had been shortened, excess of physical labour had been abridged; oppression and cruelty resulting in premature death had been checked, and the means of education and mental improvement had been made possible.

Two more legislative measures, however, were still necessary to complete his labours on behalf of the industrial classes of the country. One, successfully carried in 1867, was a Bill "For Regulating the Labour of Juveniles in Workshops." It prohibited the hiring of children under eight years of age, and regulated the hours of labour of all under thirteen; it provided for the education of all children under thirteen, placed all workshops under the provisions of the Sanitary Act of 1866, and it brought, for the first time, every branch of juvenile labour, save one, under Government supervision.

The one other scheme of amelioration remaining untouched was one that had long been in contemplation, but Lord Shaftesbury had failed to find a favourable opportunity to introduce it into the House of Lords. The question, an agricultural one relating to the cultivation of the soil, was a ticklish one to introduce into that assembly, and he reserved it to the last because it presented the greatest difficulties, and because it required all the sympathy and experience to be derived from the proofs of success furnished by the Factory Acts to obtain for it a favourable reception.

In 1863, while the Second Children's Employment Commission was sitting, Lord Shaftesbury moved an Address to the Queen praying that the Commissioners should be directed to inquire into the system of "organised" labour known by the name of Agricultural Gangs, and in April 1867, soon after the report of the Commissioners was issued, he brought the matter forward.

It was found that the system of agricultural gangs existed almost exclusively in the counties of Lincolnshire, Huntingdonshire, Cambridgeshire, Norfolk, Suffolk, and Nottinghamshire, and, to a less extent, in the counties of Northamptonshire, Bedford, and Rutland. A "gang" consisted of the gang-master and a number of women and children and young persons of both sexes, numbering from twelve to forty. The average number in the "public" gangs was twenty, that being a manageable number, employing on the whole about seven thousand boys and girls from six years old and upwards, while, in addition, there were "private" gangs employing fully twenty thousand. The public gang was under the control of an independent master, who engaged the members of the gang and contracted with the farmer to execute a certain kind and amount of agricultural work with this body of slaves; while the private gang, seldom exceeding from twelve to twenty, was in the farmer's own employ and was superintended by one of the farmer's own labourers.

The work consisted in making or keeping the land in a fit state for the growth of crops by clearing it from weeds of all kinds, spreading and putting in manure, thinning or "singling" turnips and mangold-wurzel, setting potatoes and dropping in seed for dibblers, treading corn on light soil, getting in crops when ripe—*e.g.*, pulling turnips and mangolds or beet, pulling flax and sometimes peas, instead of their being mown, topping and tailing turnips and mangolds, and such-like work.

It was usual to collect these gangs in the morning about five, each person carrying his own tools and meals, and march them off to their work at a rapid pace, sometimes a distance of four to eight miles; they would then work in the fields from eight to five or six o'clock in the evening, reaching their "homes" about nine at night.

"Year in, year out; in summer heat and winter cold; in sickness and in health; with backs warped and aching from constant stooping; with hands cracked and swollen at the back by the wind and cold and wet; with palms blistered from pulling turnips, and fingers lacerated from weeding among the stones, —these English slaves, with education neglected, with morals corrupted, degraded and brutalised, laboured from early morning till late at night, and, by the loss of all things, gained only the miserable pittance that barely kept them from starvation."

One clergyman, in giving evidence before the Commissioners, said : " Turning to the moral side of the picture, all is blank.   The benefits of education, which charity has provided, are thrown aside by the parents. The young being engaged in manual labour from morn till night, the village school is comparatively denuded of scholars.   In room of moral and religious teaching, children are auditors of obscene and blasphemous language, while also exposed to the most profligate and debased examples, thus completing the first stage of ruin.   Progressing from childhood to womanhood, the girl is brought up without experience in the management of domestic affairs, and it is no wonder that when the duties of servitude and married life are demanded of her she is ignorant of both. There is not one extensive occupier of land, nor one sober-minded person throughout my parish, who does not denounce the gangs as destructive to the morals of the poor."

With regard to the physical side of the picture, a mother, who had worked in the gangs many years, said: " Sometimes the poor children are very ill-used by the gang-master.   One has used them horribly, kicking them, hitting them with fork-handles and hurdle-sticks, and even knocking them down.   My own children have been dropped into across the loins and dropped right down, and if they don't know how to get up he has kicked them.   I have often seen my own and other children knocked about in this way. My boy, when about ten or eleven, had a white swelling on his knee, and lay suffering nearly six years before he had his leg and thigh taken off. He came back one day and said he had a thorn, but others told me about the man kicking him. He was a very quiet boy, and was for peace. The doctor said it was from ill-usage—a fall or kick ; there was no thorn."

Medical evidence was adduced to show that the mortality of young children was as great as in the most infanticidal of the large manufacturing towns ; that rheumatism was crippling the middle-aged women; that curvature of the spine was common, and, worst of all, that immorality of all kinds was prevalent to an alarming extent.

And yet no hand had been stretched out for the deliverance of these poor creatures. Once, when the question was discussed in the House of Commons, it was alleged that no legislation on the subject could be effectual ; that it would only do mischief, by depriving women of their means of subsistence ; that it would be an interference with the rights of employers—in short, most of the arguments which had been adduced against the Bill to remove women from employment in mines and collieries were again brought forward with cold, unsympathetic iteration.

These arguments Lord Shaftesbury had successfully demolished, and he laid before the House of Lords a scheme, moderate but merciful, to remedy the wrongs inflicted by the horrible " gang " system and to affect the entire agricultural population of every county. He concluded his strong indictment in these words :—

" My lords, in attempting to grapple with this evil, I hope your lordships will kindly aid me by your sympathy and support. In this way you will give the crowning stroke to the various efforts made for many years past to bring all the industrial occupations of the young and the defenceless under the protection of the law; and that, whether they are employed in trade, in manufactures, or in any handicraft whatever, every child under a certain age may be subject only to a limited amount of labour, and be certain to receive an adequate amount of education. All that remains for your lordships now to do, as representing the landowners of the kingdom, is to embrace within the scope of your beneficent legislation the whole mass of the agricultural population. Then, I believe, we shall be enabled to say that no country upon earth surpasses us in the care we take of the physical, the moral, and the educational wellbeing of the myriads of our humble fellow-creatures. My lords, the object you have in view is well worthy of all the time, the anxiety, the zeal, and the talents which can be bestowed upon it ; and I am satisfied that your lordships will earnestly desire to see it accomplished." *

The Agricultural Bill received the affirmation of the House of Lords, and, after some delay, passed into law. It was, as Lord Shaftesbury said, "the first statutory recognition of the rights of the rural children to have equal educational privileges with the children

* Shaftesbury's Speeches, p. 410.

of the towns "; it was, as he had prayed it might be, the "crowning stroke" to his lifelong efforts to bring all the occupations of the young and defenceless under the protection of the law, and it swept from the face of the land the last of the long series of evils which could be dealt with by industrial legislation.

CHAPTER VII.

CONDITION OF THE WORKING CLASSES.

FROM an early period of his career Lord Shaftesbury took an absorbing interest in the welfare of labouring men. He could not shut his eyes to the fact that they were almost universally regarded merely as a part of the machinery of the country, that they were oppressed by unjust laws, that they had no power to combine in their own defence, that artificers were prohibited from emigrating when the labour-market was overstocked, and that no efforts were being made in any direction to raise and improve them, either physically, morally, or religiously. A spirit of discontent was giving place to a spirit of lawlessness—the only argument they could use with effect in self-defence was defiance.

And, truly, the working man had cause for bitter complaint. There were no efficient educational laws in existence; industrial schools, mechanics' institutions, working-men's clubs, were unknown; the Poor Laws were pauperising and degrading; Post Office Savings Banks, the science of sanitation, a free newspaper press, limited liability, employers' liability—all these had yet to be. Crime was rampant, and there was no proper police force in existence until 1829 to grapple with it. The tastes of the people were low and coarse, and what cheap literature there was only pandered to it. The Church was in a state of lethargy, and the vast machinery of philanthropy, with which we have been familiar since the beginning of the second half of the century, was only in its infancy.

Meanwhile, the population of the country was increasing by gigantic strides—the result of the introduction of steam and new departments of commerce. In Birmingham, for example, the population in 1815 was 90,000; in 1832 it was 150,000; and in Great Britain generally it increased from about 16,500,000 in 1831 to nearly 30,000,000 in 1881, or nearly 100 per cent.*

In the early years of which we write, tens of thousands of fresh human beings crowded into our large manufacturing towns to find employment in their turn, and to lead more or less civilised lives. Quite a new phase of humanity was introduced, bringing with it new vices and many new dangers, creating a spirit of disaffection and unrest, and causing much suffering and want. The old order was changing, yielding place to the new, and it brought with it many of the evils which are inevitable in such a crisis. Of course it brought with it "new comforts, new noblenesses, new generosities, new conceptions of duty and of how that duty should

* Robert Giffen, " Progress of the Working Classes."

be done," but these things were not apparent at the time.

Moreover, as has been well said, the rapid increase of population during the first half of this century "began at a moment when the British stock was specially exhausted, namely, about the end of the long French war. . . . Year after year, till the final triumph of Waterloo, not battle only, but worse destroyers than shot and shell—fatigue and disease —had been carrying off our stoutest, ablest, healthiest young men, each of whom represented, alas! a maiden left unmarried at home, or married in default to a less able man. The strongest went to the war; each who fell left a weaklier man to continue the race, while of those who did not fall too many returned with tainted and weakened constitutions, to injure, it may be, generations yet unborn." *

It was patent to all who had eyes to see, that the children of 1830-50 were not equal, constitutionally, to their parents, nor they again to their grandparents; and this degrading process was going on most surely and most rapidly in our large towns, and was spreading in a proportionate degree to the rural districts.

Bad as was the condition of the ordinary labouring man, that of the agricultural labourer was infinitely worse. From him was exacted the maximum of toil for the minimum of wages; he was reckoned merely among the goods and chattels of his employer; his "common round" was to work and eat and drink and die

* Charles Kingsley, " Health and Education."

Even so recently as 1873, when the county franchise was under consideration, there were many who thought the subject was ill-timed; that the rural workman was an unfit subject to be invested with political power. The idea was even then prevalent that agricultural labourers had no aspirations or desires above working, eating, drinking, and sleeping, and were more than content to let their "betters" think for them, act for them, make laws for them, and administer those laws as they thought fit, without any reference to the opinion of the working man.

Subsequent events have shown that this view did not represent the true state of things: farm-labourers and others of that class who, for centuries, had been socially, morally, financially, and politically wronged, smarting under a sense of oppression, have within recent years come forward in a manly way to make their grievances known, and to demand their political and educational rights.

Lord Shaftesbury never made that broad distinction between the workman in trade and the workman in agriculture that was almost universally made. He, almost alone, had a good word for the agricultural labourer at a time when he was the most neglected of all the working classes.

"That he is a 'skilled artisan,' will any one deny?" he asked. "Look at him engaged with the plough; see the length and straightness of each furrow; its mathematical precision, the steadiness of his hand and eye, and his masterly calculation of distance and force. Observe a hedger in all the various branches of that part of labour, and admit the accuracy of judgment that is required for a calling so apparently humble. No spinner could do what he does, any more than he could do what is done by the spinner. His talk, too, may be of bullocks ; it may be also of sheep ; it may be of every parochial matter : but then it is talk upon his special vocation ; and oftentimes how sound and sensible it is ! He has not, of course, the acquirements and acuteness of the urban operative ; his labour is passed in comparative solitude, and he returns to his home at night, in a remote cottage or a small village, without the resources of clubs, mechanics' institutes, and the friction of his fellowmen. Still, he may say with the most scientific, that he is master of the profession to which he is called, and every one should rejoice to add, to this honourable and useful career, whatever is possible to comfort and adorn it."

Long before the passing of the Reform Bill of 1832 Lord Shaftesbury was keenly alive to the condition of the working classes generally, and the pressing necessity there was for an enlightened public opinion on the question, and, as Dr. Arnold termed it, "the solution of the most difficult problem ever yet proposed to man's wisdom, and the greatest triumph over selfishness ever yet required of his virtue." He saw symptoms of a universal disease spreading throughout vast masses of the people ; he saw conspiracies against God and good arising from the tyranny and injustice under which the working classes suffered ; he saw vast and inflammable masses waiting day by day for the spark to explode them into mischief.

" We cover the land with spectacles of misery," he said ; "wealth is felt only by its oppressions ; few, very few, remain in the trading districts to spend liberally the riches they have acquired ; the successful leave the field to be ploughed afresh by new aspirants after gain, who, in turn, count their periodical profits and exact the maximum of toil for the minimum of wages. No wonder that thousands of hearts should be against a system which establishes the relations, without calling forth the mutual sympathies, of master and servant, landlord and tenant, employer and employed. . . . When called upon to suggest our remedy of the evil, we reply by an exhibition of the cause of it ; the very statement involves an argument and contains its own answer within itself. Let your laws, we say to the Parliament, assume the proper functions of law ; protect those for whom neither wealth, nor station, nor age, have raised a bulwark against tyranny ; but above all, open your treasury, erect churches, send forth the ministers of religion, reverse the conduct of the enemy of mankind, and sow wheat among the tares ; all hopes are groundless, all legislation weak, all conservatism nonsense, without this Alpha and Omega of policy ; it will give content instead of bitterness, engraft obedience on rebellion, raise purity from corruption, and life from the dead." *

* From an article by Lord Ashley in the *Quarterly Review*, December 1840.

The welfare of the working classes was the object of almost every great project undertaken by Lord Shaftesbury from the beginning to the end of his career. We have glanced at some of his labours on behalf of women, children, and young persons ; we have now to look at his labours in regard to the education of the working classes and the condition of their dwellings.

In February 1843 he moved an Address to the Crown praying Her Majesty to take into her " instant and serious consideration the best means of diffusing the benefits and blessings of a moral and religious education amongst the working classes of her people."

The educational system of the country was at that time in a state of transition. From 1834 to 1839 an annual grant of £20,000 had been divided in equitable proportions between the National Society, representing the Church of England, and the British and Foreign School Society, representing the Nonconformists, and was dispensed by them for the purpose of erecting school buildings in aid of private benevolence.

In 1839, in the face of a determined opposition, the Committee of Council on Education was appointed, and the system of school inspectors, who dispensed the grants annually made by Parliament, was in 1843 in full operation. Schools, not necessarily in connection with either of the two great rival societies, had, too, been established, with the sanction of the Committee, in poor and populous places.

While acknowledging the vast and meritorious efforts of the National Society and of the Dissenting bodies, he found that there was a tremendous waste still remaining uncultivated, "a great and terrible wilderness," and he drew in strong outlines a picture of the prevailing ignorance and moral degradation in all parts of the country, and called for State interference on an unprecedented scale. Without entering upon the subjects he dealt with by statistics in the course of his remarkable speech—a speech far in advance of the times—his position may be indicated in the following extract :—

"If it be true, as most undoubtedly it is, that the State has a deep interest in the moral and physical prosperity of all her children, she must not terminate her care with the years of infancy, but extend her control and providence over many other circumstances that affect the working man's life. Without entering here into the nature and variety of those practical details which might be advantageously taught in addition to the first and indispensable elements, we shall readily perceive that many things are requisite, even to the adult, to secure to him, so far as is possible, the well-being of his moral and physical condition. I speak not now of laws and regulations to abridge, but to enlarge his freedom ; not to limit his rights, but to multiply his opportunities of enjoying them ; laws and regulations which shall give him what all confess to be his due ; which shall relieve him from the danger of temptations he would willingly avoid and under which he cannot but fall ; and which shall place him, in many aspects of health, happiness, and possibilities of virtue, in that position of independence and security from which, under the present state of things, he is too often excluded."*

Three items only of the "many practical details which might be advantageously taught" were enumerated by Lord Ashley. The first was the obnoxious truck system, which encouraged improvidence by preventing the chance of a habit of saving, as nobody could save food ; which prevented families from obtaining a sufficient supply of clothing and more comfortable furniture, in proportion to the possession of which it was always found that the working man became more steady, industrious, and careful—a system which drove the mining districts of South Wales into open rebellion in 1834, and produced the serious disturbances that took place in South Staffordshire in 1842.† The next items were the payment of wages in public-houses,‡ and the state of the dwellings of the poor.

The whole speech was full of power and statesmanlike foresight, and it was conceived in a spirit that was new to the majority of his hearers. It was spoken, too, at a time (1843) when, as he said, the

* "Speeches," p. 79.

† Many of the evils of the system were not abolished till 1887.

‡ Earl Stanhope's Bill, "To Prohibit the Payment of Wages to Workmen in Public-houses and certain other Places," taken charge of in the House of Commons by Mr. Samuel Morley, passed into law in 1881, and a system which had wrought nothing but mischief was thus swept away.

moral condition of England seemed destined by Providence to lead the moral condition of the world. "Year after year we are sending forth thousands and hundreds of thousands of our citizens to people the vast solitudes and islands of another hemisphere; the Anglo-Saxon race will shortly overspread half the habitable globe. What a mighty and what a rapid addition to the happiness of mankind, if these thousands should carry with them, and plant in those distant regions, our freedom, our laws, our morality and our religion!" His closing words, hackneyed though they are, deserve to be repeated whenever Lord Shaftesbury's life as a social reformer is set forth, as they rang out the key-notes of the "new philanthropy" for the working classes.

"We owe to the poor of our land," he said, "a weighty debt. We call them improvident and immoral, and many of them are so; but that improvidence and immorality are the results, in a great measure, of our neglect, and, in not a little, of our example. We owe them, too, the debt of kinder language and more frequent intercourse. This is no fanciful obligation: our people are more alive than any other to honest zeal for their cause, and sympathy with their necessities which, fall though it oftentimes may on unimpressible hearts, never fails to find some that it comforts, and many that it softens. Only let us declare, this night, that we will enter on a novel and a better course—that we will seek their temporal through their eternal welfare—and the half of our work will then have been achieved. There are many hearts to be won, many minds to be instructed, and many souls to be saved : *oh Patria! oh Divum domus!*—the blessing of God will rest upon our endeavours; and the oldest among us may live to enjoy, for himself and for his children, the opening day of the immortal, because the moral, glories of the British Empire."

Without pursuing in detail Lord Shaftesbury's actions in regard to the question of national education, it will be sufficient for our present purpose to say that he never departed from the principles he laid down in the speech from which we have quoted. He ever pleaded for an enlarged and comprehensive system for the instruction of the masses, and when in 1870, after large masses of the community had been invested with political power, the whole question was taken in hand by Mr. W. E. Forster, the member for Bradford, on behalf of Mr. Gladstone's Government, Lord Shaftesbury was in the forefront of the battle in strenuous opposition to the Secularists. Upon the second reading of the Bill he distinguished himself by his moderation. "Convinced that to require as a condition of State aid that the Bible should be read in all schools would be resisted, he accepted the measure with its optional enactments as to religious education as the best possible thing, having regard to the temper of Parliament. It is beyond doubt that he contributed very largely to the defeat of the Secularists, and saved the country from the scandal of a godless system of education." *

* "Shaftesbury: A New Memoir," *Record* Newspaper Office, 1885.

In considering Lord Shaftesbury's efforts to better the condition of the working classes, and especially the agricultural labourers, both as regards education and dwellings, we must not lose sight of the fact that while he was Lord Ashley he laboured under special disadvantage, from having marked out for himself, from the first, a course that met with the strong disapprobation of his father. For ten years— from 1829 to 1839—he was estranged from his father's home, and a reconciliation effected in the latter year lasted for only a brief period.

It was only to be expected that the large manufacturers, smarting under Lord Ashley's attacks on the condition of the operatives whom they employed, should ask why his charity did not begin at home. Hostile newspapers took the matter up, and even Miss Martineau wrote such words as these : " He need but have gone into the hovels of his father's peasantry to have seen misery and mental and moral destitution which could not be matched in the worst retreats of the manufacturing population." To such an extent was this persecution carried on, notwithstanding the fact that it was an open secret how the matter really stood, that Lord Ashley said in public : " The county of Dorset is in every man's mouth ; every paper, metropolitan and provincial, teems with charges against us ; we are within an ace of becoming a byword for poverty and oppression."

Stung by the censure of his unfriendly critics, he took occasion, at an agricultural meeting held at Sturminster, in Dorset, to utter what he described as

" some strong truths respecting wages, dwellings, truck, delay of payment, and exclusion from gleaning." This of course called forth the renewed anger of his father, who told him that he was exciting the people, inducing them to make extortionate demands, and that they were not easily put down when once up. " They got on very well, he did not know how, with 7s. and even 6s. a week ; their wages could not be raised, and as for their dwellings, it was very easy to point out the evil, but where was the remedy ? "

That was exactly what Lord Ashley was seeking to find out, but the task was one of extreme difficulty. If he suppressed the faults of landed proprietors, he roused the accusations of the League ; if he rebuked them, he stirred the resentment of his father.

There is an old saying that " the sting of a rebuke is in the truth of it " ; and, unfortunately, the state of affairs in Dorsetshire and on his father's estates was deplorable. " God knows," he wrote, " I have long mourned over these things, and long resolved on every self-denial rather than not remove them."

It was not until eight years after this that those estates became his, and then he set to work in right good earnest to fulfil his pledge, concentrating all his energies, not in the adornment of St. Giles' House, but in the state of the labourers and their dwellings. He inspected the cottages, and found them " filthy, close, indecent, unwholesome." " I have passed my life," he wrote, " in rating others for allowing rotten houses and immoral, unhealthy dwellings ; and now I come into an estate rife with abominations . . . and

I have not a farthing to set them right." So he borrowed money, raised mortgages, sold his plate and pictures, and after a desperate struggle, lasting for a quarter of a century, he left the village of Wimborne St. Giles a model village.

"The cottages are mostly semi-detached, and surrounded by pleasant little gardens, neatly kept and abounding in fruit trees, vegetables, and flowers. These cottages, admirable in their construction, and consisting of five or six rooms well planned for comfort, for convenience, and for health, are let at the low rent of 1s. a week, or one-sixteenth of the average wages of the labouring men who occupy them."

CHAPTER VIII.

SANITATION, AND THE DWELLINGS OF THE POOR.

IN 1838 a severe outbreak of disease occurred in the East End of London—a part of Whitechapel, situated on the borders of a large and stagnant pond, being the locality most affected. Mr. (afterwards Sir) Edwin Chadwick, then Secretary of the Poor Law Board, was applied to, and he immediately persuaded his Board to institute a Medical Commission of Inquiry. Dr. Neil Arnott, Dr. Kay (afterwards Sir Kay-Shuttleworth), and Dr. T. Southwood Smith, three of the best living authorities on sanitary science, were sent to report not only on that particular outbreak but on the sanitary condition of the Metropolis. The reports of these three pioneers became text-books on sanitation.

In 1839 came the far-famed inquiry into the health of the labouring classes of the other parts of England and Wales.

The subject was of intense interest to Lord Ashley, who had already stood forth as the pioneer of the great question which in after years was to become so conspicuous a feature of his labours—the Housing of the Poor ; and in the year 1842—the same year in which the Committee of Inquiry presented its report —he assisted in founding the " Labourers' Friend Society," afterwards known as the " Society for Improving the Condition of the Labouring Classes," the object of which was to ventilate the question of healthy homes, and to show what could be done at the smallest possible cost consistent with a fair return of interest on the capital expended.

It was in 1846, at one of the meetings of this Society—of which the Prince Consort became the president—that Lord Ashley drew public attention to the insanitary state of the dwellings of the poor, in a speech which commanded the attention of the whole country.

" I do not speak merely.from books," he said, " I do not speak merely from the accounts that have been given me ; because I have not only in past years, but during the present year, devoted a very considerable number of hours day by day to going over some of the worst localities in various parts of this great metropolis."

In the course of his peregrinations he found crowded rooms, with sometimes two or three families in a single apartment, rooms so foul and dark that they were exposed to every physical mischief that could beset the human race—without light, without water, without drainage, without ventilation ; he penetrated into courts and alleys so filthy that they outraged every sense of decency, thronged with a dense and most immoral population of every caste and grade of

9

character, defiled by perpetual habits of intoxication, amid riot, blasphemy, noise, and tumult, accompanied by every kind of indecency.

As an active step to show what might be done to remedy this mass of evil, he announced the intention of the Society "to erect in the heart of the parish of St. Giles a model lodging-house—a house where a young man coming up from the country for the first time, or others who wish to live in a place where some, at least, of the decencies of life are observed, may find a place of retirement and of shelter at a moderate rent,"*—the germ of the great Model Lodging-House system with which we are all familiar.

Anxious as Lord Ashley was to advance the question of national education, he felt satisfied that direct labours in that direction were premature until the dwellings of the poor were made fit for decent habitation.

"There is a mighty stir now made on behalf of education," he said on one occasion, and he repeated the burden of his remarks a hundred times, "and I thank God for it ; but let me ask you to what purpose it is to take a little child, a young female for instance, and teach her for six hours a day the rules of decency and every virtue, and then send her back to such abodes of filth and profligacy as to make her unlearn by the practice of one hour the lessons of a year, to witness and oftentimes to share, though at first against her will, the abominations that have been recorded.

* "Speeches," p. 216.

Gentlemen, if you desire to have a moral and well-conducted people, you must do your best to place, and to keep, them under such circumstances that they may have the means and opportunity to bring into action the lessons they have been taught, the principles they have acquired. People go to their Boards of Guardians and hear the long catalogue of bastardy cases, and they cry out 'Sluts and profligates,' assuming that, when in early life these persons have been treated as swine, they are afterwards to walk with the dignity of Christians."

The first legislative outcome of this agitation, of any permanent importance, was the Public Health Act of 1848, which he warmly supported, although he thought it was susceptible of very great improvement. Nevertheless, it was the practical beginning of the work of sanitary reform. A Board of Health was appointed, with Lord Ashley, Lord Carlisle, Mr. Edwin Chadwick, and Dr. Southwood Smith as Commissioners.

As Chairman of this Board, Lord Ashley, in conjunction with Mr. Chadwick and Dr. Southwood Smith, entered upon an unprecedented amount of labour which can never be told in detail. In October 1848 the country was thrown into a state of alarm by serious outbreaks of cholera. Between that date and October 1st, 1849, no fewer than 14,497 deaths occurred from that cause. Throughout that year Lord Ashley was working with his colleagues night and day in the very midst of the plague. Scenes of the most horrible nature were constantly before his eyes; labours of the most exhausting kind were his daily portion. He led a charmed life, as some thought; he described it thus : " Have been mercifully preserved through this pestilence. Have not, I thank God, shrunk from one hour of duty in the midst of this city of the plague, and yet it has not approached either me or my dwelling."

The result of his investigations was to prove conclusively that " wherever neglect, depression, vice or poverty pressed down the population, there the pestilence raged with its retributive and warning arm ; the sins of omission and commission were revisited on the lives of those who perpetrated or permitted them," and that " foul drains, overflowing cesspools, fetid waters, overcrowded lodging-houses, damp cellars and ill-ventilated rooms attracted the pestilence, which then spread to the houses of the better classes and to the mansions of the rich.".

The toil and anxiety entailed upon him as Chairman of the Board of Health, both during the cholera time and subsequently, in relation to measures for procuring a better water-supply, legislating for extra-mural interment, enforcing vaccination and smoke-abatement and such-like sanitary improvements, told greatly upon his health and spirits.

Every fresh measure brought fresh labour to the Board, and not only so, but it called forth the bitter hostility of every class that it was compelled to attack. The Dissenters were angry because a new Burial Bill was proposed ; Parliamentary agents became sworn enemies because their fees and general expenses were reduced within reasonable limits; civil engineers, because new principles were carried into effect by abler men and at less cost; the College of Physicians and all its dependencies, because of independent action and singular success in dealing with the cholera, many Poor Law medical officers succeeding where fashionable London doctors failed; all the Boards of Guardians, for their selfishness, cruelty, and reluctance to relieve the suffering poor had been exposed; all the Water Companies, for their systems had been weighed in the balance and found wanting, and new ones had been introduced; the Commissioners of Sewers, for their plans and principles had to be entirely reversed.

In the summer of 1854 the abolition of the Board of Health was brought about, and Lord Shaftesbury's consequent retirement, after he had given to it "five years of his life and intense labour, and had not received even the wages of a pointer, with 'That's a good dog.'" The Report published by the Board in 1854 is a document which still remains as a standard of observation, and if the Board had done no more than publish that work it would have amply vindicated itself before the country.

A few years later, when speaking at the Liverpool Social Science Congress, as President of the Health Section, Lord Shaftesbury spoke of the operation of the Public Health Act, and showed that some towns, —instancing Ely, Croydon, and Liverpool—had become nearly as healthy as the country; the reduction of mortality to seventeen in the thousand being greater than the reduction in the mortality in rural districts around them, which stood at twenty-one in the thousand ; that in Liverpool alone the new sanitary arrangements were saving 3700 lives a year as compared with former times. These considerations, he held, were but incentives to further action, seeing that the preventible mortality in the country amounted to no less than 90,000 a year, or, putting it within easy compass and calling it 40,000, meant four lives an hour ! Replying to an outcry against expense, he was always ready with the affirmation that it was disease that was expensive and health that was cheap.

It was while he was in office as Chairman of the Board of Health, namely, in April 1851, that he brought forward in the House of Commons a Bill to Encourage the Establishment of Lodging-Houses for the Working Classes, and, a few days later, a Bill for the Regulation and Inspection of Common Lodging-Houses.

We will not weary the reader with many extracts from the papers he wrote and speeches he made while collecting information on the subjects he had in hand.   Let two, out of hundreds, suffice ; the first, contributed in an article published in the *Quarterly Review*, giving a description of a hapless wanderer from the country seeking a shelter in a London lodging-house, and the other given in a speech in which he brought forward the first of the measures referred to :—

" The astonishment and perplexities of a young

person on his arrival here, full of good intentions to
live honestly, would be almost ludicrous were they
not the preludes to such mournful results. He
alights, and is instantly directed for the best accommodation to Duck Lane (Westminster), St. Giles,
Saffron Hill, Spitalfields, or Whitechapel. He
reaches the indicated region through tight avenues
of glittering fish and rotten vegetables, with door-
ways or alleys gaping on either side—which, if they
be not choked with squalid garments or sickly
children, lead the eye through an interminable vista
of filth and distress—and begins his search for the
'good entertainment.' The pavement, where there
is any, rugged and broken, is bespattered with dirt
of every hue, ancient enough to rank with the fossils,
but offensive as the most recent deposits. The
houses—small, low, and mournful—present no one
part, in windows, doorposts, or brickwork, that
seems fitted to stand for another week ; rags and
bundles stuff up the panes and defend the passages,
blackened with use and by the damps arising from
the undrained and ill-ventilated recesses. Yet each
one affects to smile with promise, and invites the
country bumpkin to the comfort and repose of
'Lodgings for Single Men.'

" He enters the first, perhaps the largest, and finds
it to consist of seven apartments of very moderate
dimensions. Here are stowed—besides children—
sixty adults, a goodly company of males and females,
of every profession of fraud and violence, with a very
few poor and industrious labourers. He turns to

another hostel—the reader will not, we know, proceed without misgivings, but we assure him our picture is drawn from real life. The *parlour* measures eighteen feet by ten. Beds are arranged on each side of it, composed of straw, rags, and shavings, all in order, but not decently according to the apostolic precept. Here he sees twenty-seven male and female adults, and thirty-one children, with several dogs (for dogs, the friends of man, do not forsake him in his most abandoned condition), in all, fifty-eight human beings in a contracted den, from which light and air are systematically excluded. He seeks the upper room, as more likely to remind him of his native hills. It measures twelve feet by ten, and contains six beds, which in their turn contain thirty-two individuals—and these bearing but little resemblance to Alexander the Great, Cujas the Lawyer, or Lord Herbert of Cherbury, whose bodies yielded naturally a fine perfume. Disgusted once more, he turns with hope to the tranquillity of a smaller tenement. Here, groping his way up an ascent more like a flue than a staircase, he finds a nest of four tiny compartments —and they are all full. It is, however, in vain to search further. The evening has set in ; the tenants are returned to their layers ; the dirt, confusion, and obscenity baffle alike tongue, pen, and paint-brush ; but if our bewildered novice would have for the night a roof over his head, he must share the floor with as many men, women, and babies as it has space for."

Our second extract is from the speech of Lord

Ashley on moving to bring in the Lodging-House
Bill. After drawing attention to the necessity that
existed for making provision for the working classes
who were turned out of their dwellings by the opening
up of new thoroughfares for the improvement of the
metropolis, he said :—

"To give a summary of the state of the country I
may mention that the Inspectors of the Board of
Health have examined 161 populous places, the
aggregate population being 1,912,599 ; and, without
exception, one uniform statement has been made with
respect to the domiciliary condition of large masses
of the workpeople—that it is of one and the same
disgusting character."

He showed how in a model lodging-house a man
could have a compartment to himself, with a bed,
chair, and space for all necessary movements, for 4d.
a night—exactly the same payment demanded from
him in the worst and most disgusting locality—and
that such a house, as evidenced by the accounts of the
Society for Improving the Condition of the Labouring
Classes, yielded to the investors the clear profit of
6½ per cent.

It was a curious circumstance that, as Lord Ashley,
he moved for two Lodging-House Bills in the House
of Commons, and, his father dying in the meantime, it
was as Lord Shaftesbury that on the very day after
he took his seat in the House of Lords he moved
the second reading of one of them—the Bill for the
Inspection and Registration of Lodging-Houses. This

measure speedily passed into law, and proved so successful in abating the monstrous evils arising from the crowding of the poorest and most helpless, amidst filth and stench, as thick as men, women, and children could be huddled together, in unventilated rooms, that it elicited from Charles Dickens the praise of being the best Act ever passed by an English Legislature.

In that same year the second measure—the Bill to Encourage the Establishment of Lodging-Houses— also passed into law ; but, owing to its mutilation in passing through the House of Commons, it was only to a very limited extent put into practice, and in course of time became a dead letter.

Two years later (1853) Lord Shaftesbury took in hand a Bill to provide accommodation for the poor who were turned out of their homes by the operations of " Improvement Companies," and obtained a Committee of Inquiry ; at the same time he procured further legislation to bring common lodging-houses under more thorough inspection and control, so as to throw broad daylight into those dens in which nine-tenths of the crimes perpetrated in the metropolis were planned and plotted.

There is little need to dwell in detail upon the various stages of Lord Shaftesbury's labours with regard to sanitary legislation up to this point.* The *Times* summed them up in an admirable article at this date,† in which it said : " To purify the Inferno

---

* See Hansard Debates, cxxv. 400 ; cxxvi. 1291 ; cxviii. 235 , cxxvii. 294 ; clvii., clviii.

† *Times*, May 16th, 1853

that reeks about us in this metropolis, to recover its inmates, and to drive the incorrigible nucleus into more entire insulation, is one of the labours to which Lord Shaftesbury has devoted his life; and we can never be sufficiently obliged to him for undertaking a task which, besides its immediate disagreeableness, associates his name with so much that is shocking and repulsive.

"To Lord Shaftesbury's legislation we owe the gratifying fact that these recesses are explored by authorised persons, that houses are no longer permitted to take in more than as many as can breathe properly in them, that lodging in cellars is prohibited, that the rooms are properly cleaned and white-washed, that ventilation, lighting, and drainage are provided for, and the furniture of the houses sufficient for the authorised number of lodgers. As far as the work has proceeded, we can hardly conceive a more meritorious or more gratifying triumph. It is a great result out of the very worst materials. To change a city from clay to marble is nothing compared with a transformation from dirt, misery, and vice to cleanliness, comfort, and at least a decent morality."

It will be well now to glance, very rapidly, at some of the innumerable movements which resulted from this agitation. Sanitary questions, of which Lord Shaftesbury saw the dawn and had all the early labours, passed into "Imperial" subjects. Boards were everywhere, laws were enacted, public attention roused, and ministers declared themselves prepared to bring to bear on them the whole force of Government.

The matter of the dwellings of the poor in like manner passed from individuals to companies, speculators, and finally into the regions of "Imperialism." But every effort advanced the common cause, and it is sufficient for our present purpose to mention the great organisation of Sir Sydney Waterlow and the more humble, but not less useful, efforts of Miss Octavia Hill; the erection of the Peabody Dwellings, and afterwards the institution of those suburban cities at Shaftesbury Park, Noel Park, and Queen's Park, and scores of kindred undertakings which have sprung up all over the country.

Then came the great agitation of 1883-4, when the Royal Commission on the Housing of the Poor was appointed, with the Prince of Wales as its most active member, culminating in Lord Salisbury's Act of 1885 —the "Housing of the Working Classes Act."

It was invaluable to the Commissioners to have at the outset the evidence of Lord Shaftesbury, and they had the good sense to make large use of his "sixty years' experience" of the subject in forming their conclusions. They recognised that he was without doubt the first living authority on the housing of the poor.

When the Report of the Commissioners was published it was found that there was nothing in it with regard to the state of the "slums" that had not been said before—it added nothing to the stock of knowledge of those who had previously examined into the matter. But it gave generous acknowledgment of the enormous advance which had been made during the previous half-century towards a solution of the great problem, and it furnished a full insight into the estimation in which Lord Shaftesbury's labours were held.

Quite early in his career Lord Shaftesbury was known generally as " The Working Man's Friend," and never did any man prove more emphatically his claim to the title. He recognised in them the men who have made our country what it is—to whom the nation owes a debt of boundless gratitude ; the men who have tilled our fields, cut our canals, built our cities, laid down our railroads, melted our iron, dived into the earth and brought up millions of wealth to the surface, and yet, until he espoused their cause, had been the least considered and the least cared for of any part of the population. Everything, therefore, that made it more easy and more pleasant to live— every sanitary reform, prevention of plague, medical discovery, drainage of soil, improvement in dwelling-houses, every reformatory school, every hospital, every cure of drunkenness, every movement, in short, which tended to sweeten, brighten, and prolong life—received his hearty co-operation and support for their sakes.

We think that no one, at this time of day, will question the wisdom of Lord Shaftesbury's method— first to provide a decent home, and then to provide a judicious education. So far, much has been done in both directions ; and now men have to be taught how to mend their own matters of their own reason and their own free-will, as arbiters of their own destinies, and, to a large extent, of their children's after them. They must be taught not only that they ought to be free, but that they *are* free, whether they know it or not, for good and for evil.

We must teach both them and their children the value of healthy homes, of personal cleanliness, of pure air and pure water, of various kinds of food as each tends to make bone, fat, or muscle ; the value of various kinds of clothing and physical exercise, of a free and equal development of the brain power without undue strain in any one direction, and of the causes of zymotic disease, consumption, scrofula, dipsomania ; in short, that soundest of practical sciences—the science of physiology as applied to health.

It is well to call attention to these subjects with marked emphasis, for no one can shut his eyes to the fact that town is being added to town with marvellous rapidity; that every year the population of these islands is becoming a town one ; that annually more and more human beings are engulfed by the advancing tide of buildings, and become absorbed in endless streets and courts and alleys ; that fresh air and the means of wholesome exercise are daily being withdrawn from larger and larger numbers of people ; that crowded streets and ill-ventilated dwellings produce vitiated air ; that the want of a proper supply of oxygen and of means of obtaining healthy exercise weakens the human system ; and that daily and hourly a large number of men and women, conscious of impaired vitality, resort to the spendthrift habit of drawing upon capital to replace income by permanently injuring their constitutions for the sake of the transitory stimulus which is obtained through the use of alcoholic liquors.

"The truth is," says a philanthropist in one of our monthly reviews,* "that our eyes are blinded to the evil effects of overcrowding by reason of the continued stream of fresh blood which is ever flowing from the more healthy districts into our towns, thus hindering and delaying the natural physical decay of the constitutions of the inhabitants of the latter, which would otherwise be more rapid, and consequently more apparent. If we could establish a thoroughly efficient blockade of our large cities, and allow no further emigration into them from the country, it would not be many years before the mortality in our centres of population, as compared with that in healthier districts, would be so marked, and the physical deterioration in our city population would become so apparent, that we should be forced to take immediate steps to prevent their utter annihilation."

* Lord Brabazon, *Nineteenth Century*, vol. x., p. 84.

CHAPTER IX.

RAGGED SCHOOLS.

NO account of Lord Shaftesbury as a social reformer would be even tolerably complete which omitted to notice his labours on behalf of Ragged Schools. Forty years after he had given the best of his time and talents to their advocacy, he wrote : " If my life should be prolonged for another year, and if, during that year, the Ragged School system were to fall, I should not die in the course of nature, I should die of a broken heart."

It was in 1843 that, by chance, he came across an advertisement headed " Ragged Schools," being an appeal on behalf of an experimental school which had been opened for gutter children in an unsavoury spot known municipally as Field Lane, but popularly styled " Jack Ketch's Warren," from the largeness of its annual contribution to the gallows.

A " Ragged School "—the name was given by Charles Dickens—was really what Lord Shaftesbury had been looking and hoping for, and he at once replied to the advertisement. The promoters forthwith waited upon him and explained fully their scheme for helping the neglected, destitute, and criminal children of the metropolis; and without delay he threw himself into the effort to multiply such schools, and eventually to bind them together in corporate union.

This enterprise led him into the heart of the vilest rookeries—happily unknown in the present day—to find places where such schools might be opened, and to hunt up the young arabs of the gutter to fill them ; and often might he be seen sitting amid the tattered outcasts, speaking to them kindly words of admonition and encouragement.

Those who only know the Ragged Schools of to-day can hardly conceive of what they were in the forties. The graphic pen of Charles Dickens has painted from the life the very school to which the memorable advertisement referred, and which was the scene of Lord Shaftesbury's earliest labours.

" I found my first school," he says, "in an obscure place called West Street, Saffron Hill, pitifully struggling for life under every disadvantage. It had no means; it had no suitable rooms ; it derived no power or protection from being recognised by any authority; it attracted within its walls a fluctuating swarm of faces—young in years, but youthful in nothing else—that scowled Hope out of countenance It was held in a low-roofed den, in a sickening atmosphere, in the midst of taint, and dirt, and pestilence ; with all the deadly sins let loose, howling and shrieking at the doors. Zeal did not supply the place of method and training; the teachers knew little of their office; the pupils, with an evil sharpness, found them out, got the better of them, derided them, made blasphemous answers to Scriptural questions, sang, fought, danced, robbed each other— seemed possessed of legions of devils. The place was stormed and carried over and over again ; the lights were blown out, the books strewn in the gutters, and the female scholars carried off triumphantly to their old wickedness. With no strength in it but its purpose, the school stood. it all out and made its way. Some two years since I found it quiet and orderly, full, lighted with gas, well whitewashed, numerously attended and thoroughly established."

The history of that school was typical of dozens of others planted in the vilest and most disreputable parts of London. Within ten years of its establishment, thanks in great measure to Lord Shaftesbury's influence, the Committee were able to report that they had established "a free day school for infants ; an evening school for youths and adults engaged in daily occupation; a women's evening school, for improving character and extending domestic usefulness, thereby making better mothers and more comfortable homes ; industrial classes, to teach youths tailoring and shoemaking; employment in the shape of wood chopping, as an industrial test for recommendation to situations ; a home for boys when first engaged in places, apart from unwholesome contamination ; a night refuge for the utterly desti-

tute ; a clothing society for the naked ; a distribution
of bread to the starving ; baths for the filthy ; a room
to dry clothes worn in the rain during the day ;
Bible-classes, under voluntary teaching, through which
nearly ten thousand persons of all ages, but of one
class—all in a state of physical and spiritual destitution
—had heard set forth the glad tidings of salvation ;
various prayer-meetings, quarterly conferences for committee and teachers for minute examination into the
detailed working of the institution ; a school missionary
to supply the spiritual wants of the sick, to scour the
streets, to bring youthful wanderers to the school, and
to rescue fallen females from paths of sin ; and a
Ragged Church for the proclamation of the Gospel
and the worship of God ! "

Excellent as all this was, and encouraging as an
example of what might be done, it was as nothing in
comparison with what was needed for the tens of
thousands of waifs and strays distributed throughout
the metropolis. One of the first active steps of Lord
Shaftesbury in connection with the movement was,
therefore, to visit the slums of the great city in order
to find out the extent of the evil to be dealt with.
He found that everywhere " they swarmed the streets ;
they gambolled in the gutters ; they, haunted the
markets in search of cast-away food ; they made
playgrounds of the open spaces ; they lurked under
porches of public buildings in hot and wet weather ;
and they crept into stables or under arches for their
night's lodging. They lived as the pariah dog lives,
and were treated much in the same way ; everybody

exclaimed against the nuisance, but nobody felt it to be his business to interfere."

Up to this time each Ragged School (and there were not many) had an isolated and independent existence, and it was borne in on the heart of one Mr. R. S. Starey, one of the early workers in the movement, that it would be desirable to call together all the superintendents and teachers of these isolated schools and set before them the benefits that might accrue if they were to unite together in one common society. Accordingly, in 1844, forty superintendents and teachers met in a hayloft over a cowshed in the very centre of what was then known as the Rookery of St. Giles, and then and there this little band of heroic workers formed themselves into the now world-known "Ragged School Union." Six months later Lord Ashley was elected President of the Union, an office he retained till the end of his days.

It was soon found that union was strength, and that the public association of his name with the movement was an incalculable advantage. But the duty was undertaken at an enormous cost. The toil which the success of the movement entailed grew to extraordinary dimensions. When there were more than a hundred schools affiliated to the Union, and each on its anniversary claimed his presence to preside, make a speech and distribute prizes, it may be imagined how great was the addition made to the demands on his strength and time.

But he seems never to have known what weariness meant in any work in which he was deeply interested ;

and though, as he said, " the ragged children were never out of his thoughts night and day," though he delivered thousands of speeches on their behalf, though he wandered day by day in reeking courts and alleys repulsive to every sense, though his house was invaded at all hours by secretaries of societies, teachers, superintendents, even the ragged poor themselves, he never grew weary in his work, even though, as we have seen, he had at the same time great legislative measures on hand demanding continued alertness of every faculty. It was said of him that he spoke on each of the hundred subjects in which he was interested with so much vigour and earnestness as to give the impression that the matter occupying his thought at the moment was the one hobby of his life ; but those who knew him best perceived in every utterance on behalf of Ragged Schools a depth of sympathy and tenderness, a restful satisfaction, an inspiring hope which no other work seemed to afford him in an equal degree.

A great impetus was given to the movement by the publication of an article from his pen on " Ragged Schools," in which he described the habits and surroundings of the queer mortals,—"who look not like th' inhabitants o' the earth, and yet are on't,"—the objects of his solicitude. He says :—

" It is a curious race of beings that these philanthropists have taken in hand. Every one who walks the streets of the metropolis must daily observe several members of the tribe, bold, and pert, and dirty as

London sparrows, but pale, feeble, and sadly inferior
to them in plumpness of outline. Their business, or
pretended business, seems to vary with the locality.
At the West End they deal in lucifer matches,
audaciously beg, or tell a touching tale of woe. Pass
on to the central parts of the town, to Holborn or
the Strand, and the regions adjacent to them, and you
will there find the numbers greatly increased; a few
are pursuing the avocations above mentioned of their
more Corinthian fellows; many are spanning the
gutters with their legs, and dabbling with earnestness
in the latest accumulation of nastiness, while others,
in squalid and half-naked groups, squat at the
entrances of the narrow, fetid courts and alleys that
lie concealed behind the deceptive frontages of
our larger thoroughfares. Whitechapel and Spitalfields teem with them like an ants' nest; but it is
in Lambeth and in Westminster that we find the
most flagrant traces of their swarming activity. There
the foul and dismal passages are thronged with
children of both sexes, and of every age from three
to thirteen. Though wan and haggard, they are
singularly vivacious, and engaged in every sort of
occupation but that which would be beneficial to
themselves and creditable to the neighbourhood.
Their appearance is wild; the matted hair, the disgusting filth that renders necessary a closer inspection
before the flesh can be discerned between the rags
which hang about it, and the barbarian freedom
from all superintendence and restraint, fill the mind
of a novice in these things with perplexity and

dismay. Visit these regions in the summer, and you are overwhelmed by the exhalations; visit them in the winter and you are shocked by the spectacle of hundreds shivering in apparel that would be scanty in the tropics; many are all but naked; those that are clothed are grotesque : the trousers, where they have them, seldom pass the knee; the tail-coats very frequently trail below the heels. In this guise they run about the streets and line the banks of the river at low water, seeking coals, sticks, corks, for nothing comes amiss as treasure-trove; screams of delight burst occasionally from the crowds, and leave the passer-by, if he be in a contemplative mood, to wonder and to rejoice that moral and physical degradation have not yet broken every spring of their youthful energies."

The movement grew with rapidity; the children flocked to the schools, sometimes it may be for the sake of the light and warmth and shelter, oftener perhaps for the fun of the thing, but still they came, and with them a staff of manly men and brave women who gave their time, their money, and their talents gratuitously and ungrudgingly to the work. Questions relating to the immediate education and relief of street arabs soon gave place to larger and wider questions—how they were to be employed, what was to be their future.

It was found that between 1840 and 1847 youthful crime had increased to an enormous extent. Youths, whose ages ranged from fourteen to twenty-four, were shown to constitute less than a tenth of the population, while in point of fact they committed no less than a fourth part of the crime. It was stated on authority that in London alone there were over thirty thousand " naked, filthy, roaming, lawless, and deserted children, quite distinct from the ordinary poor."

To let these alone was to ensure that they would not let society alone hereafter. The quick-eyed, ragged urchin who could successfully withdraw an article from a window stall and transfer it to his trousers' pocket, would, in all probability, be a desperate burglar in a few years if his present pilfering were not prevented. He needed but little practice to master the easy rule of progression in crime. " For example," says a practical philanthropist, " a young acquaintance of ours graduated in a fortnight from stealing twopence to taking a paraffin lamp, and from taking a paraffin lamp to driving off in a horse and cart not his own. And when, from constant practice, the child's nimble fingers have attained dexterity in the art of thieving, he will not only brag of his exploits among his young companions, but also initiate them in the tricks of his trade. Thus he becomes 'captain' of a gang of child-rogues, who drink in with avidity his thrilling tales of hair-breadth escapes from shopmen's and policemen's clutches, and eagerly covet similar experiences. Some follow him chiefly from that boyish love of adventure which a career of petty theft furnishes so many opportunities to gratify, while others join the band simply to satisfy the natural craving of empty stomachs for food otherwise not forthcoming."

It was in order to rescue the deserving from the contamination of such, and other, influences, that in June 1848 Lord Ashley brought forward a motion in the House of Commons, "That it is expedient that means be annually provided for the voluntary emigration to some one of Her Majesty's colonies of a certain number of young persons, of both sexes, who have been educated in the schools ordinarily called 'Ragged Schools,' in and about the metropolis." He stated that with the aid of the London City Mission 1600 street arabs had been placed under examination, of whom 162 confessed that they had been in prison not once nor twice—many of them several times; 116 had run away from their homes, the result, in many instances, of ill-treatment; 170 slept in lodging-houses—nests of every abomination that the mind of man can conceive; 253 confessed that they lived altogether by begging; 216 had neither shoes nor stockings; 280 had no hats, caps, or head-covering; 101 had no linen; 219 never slept in beds; 68 were the children of convicts; 125 had step-mothers, to whom may be traced much of the misery that drives the children of the poor to the commission of crime; 306 had lost one or both parents, a large proportion having lost both.

Even more startling was the statement, compiled from the reports of the metropolitan police, that in the previous year (1847) there were taken into custody 62,181 persons of all ages and of both sexes. Of these 20,702 were females, and 41,479 were males; whereof there were under twenty years of age 15,698; between ten and fifteen, 3,682; under ten, 362. Of the whole 62,000, 22,075 could neither read nor write, and 35,227 could read only, or read and write imperfectly. Out of these 62,000 persons taken into custody there were no less than 28,118 who had no business, trade, calling, or occupation whatsoever.

Lord Ashley's proposal, in order to stimulate the Ragged School system, was that the Government should agree to take every year from these schools say 1000 children—500 boys and the same number of girls—and transplant them at the public expense to South Australia, the colony at that time making the greatest demand for labour. The response of the Government was a grant of £1500 for an experimental trial of the scheme, and this, aided by contributions of friends, placed Lord Ashley in a position to launch it.

From its inception the scheme was a success, "Lord Ashley's boys" soon became a demand in the colonies, and the most gratifying accounts were received of their behaviour under the altered circumstances of their lives. Yet, strange to say, when in the following year Lord Ashley narrated in the House of Commons the story of the success of the scheme, the House refused a further grant, and henceforth emigration was promoted from private sources.

Although we cannot follow in detail the marvellous developments and amplifications of the Ragged School

Union, we must at least glance at a few. In November 1850, in view of the Great Exhibition of the following year, a band of Ragged School teachers met at Field Lane to consider how they might obtain employment for some of their scholars when London would be crowded with visitors from all parts of the world. Various simple industries were considered, such as wood-chopping and mat-making, and so far the matter ended. But as four of the teachers * were walking arm-in-arm up the middle of Holborn Hill on their way home, one of them made the suggestion, " Why should we not employ shoe-blacks in the streets of London as they do in various foreign cities ? "

The idea was snapped at, each subscribed 10*s.* on the spot—the price of a uniform and apparatus for four boys—500 circulars were sent out, and the first and only reply came as follows :—

" DEAR MACGREGOR,—Good idea. Carry it out. I will give you £5.

" Yours sincerely,
" ASHLEY."

The scheme was successful beyond all anticipation. Lord Ashley became president of the society, " stations " were assigned to the boys ; Sir George Cornewall Lewis, then Chancellor of the Exchequer,

---

* The four teachers were John MacGregor (Rob Roy), J. R. Fowler, R. J. Snape, and F. S. Reilly (afterwards Sir Francis Reilly, K.C.M.G.).

obtained the insertion of a clause in an Act of Parliament whereby street shoeblacks were henceforward to be regarded as functionaries to be regulated and protected by the police. From the outset the earnings of the boys were divided into three parts : one part went into the boy's own pocket, one part to the society's fund for working expenses, and one part to the boys' bank. The philanthropic enterprise now extends to the whole kingdom. Thousands of boys have been trained under its auspices, but at their own cost, who, but for its instrumentality, would probably have drifted into the criminal classes. The wise forethought which prompted the founders of this society to dispose of the earnings of the boys into equal proportions has been the rule to this day. "Unlike many societies, which flourish for a season and then begin gradually to wither away, this has maintained its robust and healthy growth, and every year the earnings have steadily increased, until in 1892 they reached, merely for shoeblacking, the sum of £75,800 The present income of the brigade in London alone is over £1000 a month." *

Another important organisation sprang out of the Ragged School Union—namely, the establishment of refuges and industrial classes. The old complaint upon which Lord Shaftesbury had so often harped when speaking upon education and the dwellings of the poor—that it was useless to educate young people for a few hours in the day and then send them back

* "Life of John MacGregor" (Rob Roy), p. 86.

to filthy homes and immoral influences—applied with special force to the children of the Ragged Schools. It was found that the work in these schools "lost much of its moral power in consequence of the constant and daily antagonism it encountered from the exposure of the scholars, on retiring from the scene of instruction, to all that was contaminating and vile in the wretched places they called their homes. Lessons of virtue were nullified by examples of vice." Special and successful efforts were therefore made to provide refuges not in the metropolis only, but in the large towns and cities of the kingdom. These were of two kinds : night refuges for casual vagrants, preference being given to children attending Ragged Schools, and permanent refuges for the support and education, for a stated period, of young persons between ten and sixteen years. In this work Lord Shaftesbury, as president of the Reformatory and Refuge Union, took an absorbing interest, and an enormous amount of good was accomplished. It was to the refuge work, however, that he devoted his chief attention ; in reformatory work others were more prominent.

The intention of the industrial classes was rather to assist in the formation of tidy and useful habits than to rear a race of regular artisans. " In some of the classes, making and mending their own clothes was the only thing taught to the children ; in others, making and printing paper bags, printing handbills and circulars, making mats and church hassocks, and other simple handicrafts."

This movement, no doubt, led up to the Industrial School system, which came under the jurisdiction of the Home Office Department, and played an important part in the dimunition of juvenile crime, which has decreased during the last thirty years no less than 75 per cent.

No words of praise can be too high, and no fear of exaggeration can be entertained in speaking of the wide usefulness of two other developments of the Ragged School movement—namely, the National Refuges for Homeless and Destitute Children, and the Training Ships. Of the former, the late Mr. William Williams, a man of indomitable zeal and of great courage, intelligence, and activity, was the prime mover, and remained at the head of the movement until his death.

The institution of the training ships was a happy inspiration of Lord Shaftesbury's. In February 1866 the lads in the casual wards of workhouses and other similar places were invited to a supper at St. Giles' Refuge, Great Queen Street, Lincoln's Inn Fields. Four hundred were invited ; only 150 were present, some of the absentees excusing themselves on the ground that they " thought it was a trap," and others, more practical, that they thought " they would get lots of jaw and nothing to eat." After supper a meeting was held, when Lord Shaftesbury asked them the question, " Supposing that there were in the Thames a big ship, large enough to contain a thousand boys, would you like to be placed on board to be taught trades, or trained for the navy and the merchant service?" A unanimous shout in the affirmative was the reply.

The *Times* took the matter up; the Committee of the Boys' Refuge discussed it, and it was resolved to petition the Government for a useless ship of war and fit it up for homeless boys who wished to follow a seafaring life, and at the same time to acquire a house with about fifty acres of land where boys, not fitted for the sea, could be trained in agricultural pursuits, and so be qualified for colonial life.

The Government granted the *Chichester*, a fifty-gun frigate, which had never been out of dock, and so rapidly extended the good work on board that in 1874 the *Arethusa* was granted for the same purpose. In due course the Farm and Shaftesbury schools at Bisley, and Fortescue House at Twickenham were opened for the training of boys for colonial life; Girls' Refuges were established at Sudbury and Ealing; other organisations were set on foot, and the "National Refuges for Homeless and Destitute Children" continue to this day an honour and a blessing to the country.

On laying the foundation stone of the new buildings of the Central Boys' and Girls' Refuge at Manchester, in June 1883, Lord Shaftesbury, in his speech, said he was "glad to see they had been directing their efforts towards the training ship at Liverpool, the like of which we had many in our different ports. He believed these training ships would conduce more to the welfare of England and the honour of their country than almost anything he had ever known.

Our mercantile marine was now supplied almost entirely by foreigners, and the object of these training ships was to have it supplied by native-born subjects, men who in case of exigency—in case of war, which God forbid !—would be able to furnish our military marine with true patriotic British soldiers to defend our shores from insult and aggression. It was a noble training, too, for the lads, and showed what might be done among the destitute, among the most degraded and miserable. He had always maintained, and his long experience proved it, that the deeper we go the brighter the jewels we bring from the depths to which we descend. He was satisfied that among the great mass of the poorer classes there were some of the noblest spirits, if only they were brought to the surface and trained in the fear of God."

In a recent article* Earl Compton, the present president of the Ragged School Union, says :

" For years the education of the children was carried on in the Ragged Schools, until a national system was adopted. But even then the work of the Union could not stop ; for while secular teaching was no longer wanted, religious training and secular instruction remained as necessary as ever. No national system can supply the spiritual and physical needs of the children of the poor, many thousands of whom are even now only half-clad in winter, many are shoeless and many are half-starved. As our ideas progress the wants of child-life increase. Thus it is

* *The Quiver*, April 1897.

that after fifty-two years the work is greater and the workers are as much needed as in the commencement. It is to meet this necessity that more than 5000 voluntary helpers are now labouring amongst, and in touch with, 50,000 of London's poorest children.

" Free breakfasts, penny dinners, soup suppers are given to the hungry children, and none know better than the School Board teachers how many are half-starved when they arrive at school, and what little prospect they have of a meal during the day. . . . Thousands are sent, under proper management, for a day in the country; and what is better, many a sickly child picks up strength by a fortnight's stay in one of the Holiday Homes."

One of the latest developments of the work of the Ragged School Union is the attention which is being paid to poor crippled children, of whom there are now no fewer than 6000 on the books.

Of the schools affiliated, at the present time, (1897), to the Union, there are 192 separate buildings where 253 afternoon and evening Sunday Schools are held, with an average attendance of 50,000 children and 4887 teachers. Only 79 of all the workers receive salaries, and these give *all* their time. In addition there are 8 Day Schools, with an average attendance of over 1800; 53 Night Schools, with 2400; 116 Industrial Classes, with 4700; 198 Special Religious Services, with 15,567; 232 Bible-classes, with 4523; 131 Mothers' Meetings, with 9298; 204 Prayer

Meetings, with 9200 ; 171 Bands of Hope, with 13,067 members ; 97 School Libraries ; 70 Penny Banks, with 21,000 depositors and over £11,665 deposited ; 119 Men's and Lads' Clubs, Gymnasia, etc., with 3500 members, and Recreation Classes, etc., for 2200 members.

" The Ragged School Union," says Earl Compton in conclusion, " by its businesslike, quiet, and zealous labours, has gained the good wishes and respect of all who have gone deeply into the question of the training of our young ; and no agency could be less spared than the one which takes to its heart and cares for the most neglected and the most wretched."

CHAPTER X.

MULTUM IN PARVO.

IN the preceding chapters we have attempted to describe the main public achievements of Lord Shaftesbury. Let us now turn to some of his minor but, in many respects, not less important, labours in a less public sphere ; glancing first at those relating to religion, and next at those connected with social philanthropies and reforms.

It must be understood, at the outset of our remarks on the first head, that Lord Shaftesbury was an Evangelical Churchman, of the old school of Evangelicals, bitterly hostile to Roman Catholicism, and antagonistic to the Oxford movement in every phase of its manifold ramifications. He believed in original sin and the necessity of a " new birth " to righteousness ; in Justification by Faith as the very life of the Bible and the key of the Reformation ; in the inspiration of the Holy Scriptures from Genesis to Revelation —" from the very first syllable to the last " ; in Divine Providence as guiding every incident in human life, however inexplicable ; in direct answers to prayer ; in appropriating, by faith and love, the merits of the Lord Jesus Christ. These views, branded by many as narrow, he held from early youth till his death, never deviating from them by a hair's breadth. He was brought much into contact, and willingly, with the evangelists and philanthropists of Nonconformity ; he gave as wide a berth as he could to Ritualists, for whom he prayed, " O Lord, deliver the Church of these men, who, while their hearts are in the Vatican, still eat the bread of the Establishment and undermine her"; and he had no sympathy with the Broad Church, whose creed he denominated Neology.

Every organisation that had for its object the carrying out of the principles of the Reformation, every bulwark of backbone Protestantism, found in Lord Shaftesbury a warm-hearted supporter. To his view the stability of the Constitution, the true progress of the nation, the well-being of the people, all hung upon faithfulness to these principles. For more than half a century he was regarded as the lay leader of the Low Church party—although he himself repudiated the title—and in Parliament, on the platform, and in the press he was engaged in almost unceasing controversy with the Church of Rome and the High Church party on the one hand, and the Broad Church party on the other.

Although it is true that in 1829—three years after he entered Parliament he voted in favour of Catholic Emancipation, he had special reasons for doing so. " At first I voted against it," he wrote, " but when Peel and Wellington took it up, and showed the necessity for it, I saw that resistance was impossible. It was a subject that was always coming up; it stood in the way of everything. So, although I voted against it at first, when Peel and Wellington changed I changed, and recorded my vote for Emancipation as a member of the Commons and of the Government."

A remarkable entry in his diary some years later on, shows his feeling with regard to the matter :—

"*April 8th*, 1835.—It is a sign, a fearful sign of retributive justice, that every great question involving the existence of principles, the safety of institutions, and the stability of Governments, has now *for five years* been determined by majorities equal to, or less than, the numbers admitted from the ranks of Popery to the privileges of members of Parliament. The other night the division was carried by thirty-three, the precise number of Papists in the House of Commons!"

It was a matter of course that he persistently opposed the grant to the Maynooth Roman Catholic College in Ireland, a subject which, in 1845 and onwards, made an unprecedented stir in Protestant circles. He took exception to the grant on the ground that it was encouraging the Roman Catholic religion, fostering its colleges where that religion was taught, and endowing its priesthood—involving concession of principle without corresponding benefit.

The Papal Aggression, as it was called, of 1850

caused Lord Ashley to stand forth as the acknowledged champion of Protestantism.   A Papal Bull
had been published abolishing the administration of
Roman Catholics in England by Vicars Apostolic,
and appointing instead two Archbishops and twelve
Bishops, with territorial districts.   Dr. Wiseman was
raised to the dignity of Cardinal, and was appointed
the first Archbishop of Westminster.   He forthwith
issued a pastoral, heading it "From out of the
Flaminian Gate at Rome," and this notorious letter,
full, it must be confessed, of arrogant assumption,
ignored the Church of England, and spoke as though
England had been restored to the Roman Communion,
and would henceforth be ecclesiastically governed by
the new hierarchy.

This "aggression," coupled with the rapid rise and
spread of Puseyism and the secession of notable men
to the Church of Rome, caused a sensation and an
activity such as had never been known before and
will probably never be known again.   The Ecclesiastical Titles Act of 1851 was the Parliamentary
outcome of the agitation, and was introduced by the
Government of the day to render the assumption of
these titles illegal.   As everybody knows, the Act did
not please anybody or accomplish anything, and in
course of time good Protestants made no objection to
the assumed ecclesiastical titles, and the Act remained
a dead letter for twenty years, when it was at length
repealed.

In this, as in many other controversies, Lord Ashley
was constant in his saying, "We wage no war upon

the Roman Catholics of these realms, but we wage interminable war against the Pope and his Cardinals."

In 1851 the Protestant Alliance was formed, and Lord Ashley became its energetic president. The object of the Society was, and is, to establish union among Evangelical Protestants, and to maintain and defend against all encroachments of Popery the Scriptural doctrines of the Reformation and the principles of religious liberty as the best security for the temporal and spiritual welfare of the kingdom.

As a Church Reformer Lord Shaftesbury rendered important services. So early as 1836 he became identified with the Church Pastoral Aid Society. At its inauguration seventy clergymen met to "consider a plan for extending the means of grace in and to necessitous parishes in strict conformity with the spirit, constitution, and discipline of the Established Church." The result of the meeting, at which Lord Ashley presided, was the formation of the Society, "for the purpose of benefiting the population of our own country by increasing the number of working clergymen in the Church of England, and encouraging the appointment of pious and discreet laymen as helpers to the clergy in duties not ministerial."

Although it was patent to everybody that there was at that time a lamentable lack of clergymen to minister to the densely crowded districts of the country, and that there was a crying need for pastoral aid, much controversy ensued as to the nature of the lay help that should be given, some contending that it should be limited to candidates for holy orders who had completed their university course and were waiting for ordination, while others were opposed altogether to the introduction into the Church of a new order of lay teachers not amenable to ecclesiastical authority. Notwithstanding formidable opposition from many quarters, the Society decided "to assist, as it might be able, in the supply to destitute places of lay agents, whether candidates for holy orders or others, or whether partially or wholly to be maintained, which lay agents shall act under the direction of the incumbent, and be removable at his pleasure."

For over sixty years the Society has been in existence, and throughout his life Lord Shaftesbury gave to its operations the best of his time and talents. He presided, almost without a break, at its popular annual meeting, and it has been said that his speeches on these occasions "give the religious history of nearly half a century."

The employment of the laity for spiritual work always had the warm advocacy of Lord Shaftesbury. In the splendid work of the London City Mission he took a special interest. Although the Society was founded in 1835, it was not until ten years later that he was publicly identified with it, and then it was as a debtor to the Society, for he was wont to confess that without its aid he could never have prosecuted his inquiries into the state of the dwellings of the poor, or of the state of misery and moral degradation in which they were living. He admired the devoted lives of the missionaries and their unwearying solicitude to bring the glad tidings of the Gospel into the homes of the poor and neglected. "These men," he said, "go out day by day taking God's Word in all its simplicity, not charged, as many are, with Hebrew and Greek and Latin, and the higher criticism and 'all that dreadful nonsense'; they go out with nothing but a deep, living knowledge of the Word of God, and see what marvellous achievements have been wrought thereby." And truly these "Spiritual Police of London," as he called this army of missionaries, have made the hearts of tens of thousands to rejoice in living better lives, in better homes, and with a comfortable sense that they are not left alone in the world, but that some at least care for their state.

In like manner he admired and supported the work of the Open Air Mission. Such religious services he regarded as perfectly normal, seeing that the earliest preaching of the Gospel was in the open air; and they were certainly ecclesiastical, as the Bishops were wont at one time to preach at Paul's Cross. He was himself an occasional preacher, and it was through his instrumentality that the worthy Archbishop Tait was induced to preach on the steps of the Royal Exchange. "I believe," said Lord Shaftesbury, "that if you go and speak to the people daily and hourly the simple Word of God, you will be astonished at the thousands that will rally round the preacher, and at the mighty effects he will produce." Mighty effects were produced, multitudes were led to lead quiet and peaceable lives, bad habits were abandoned, and a new tone was given to the religious life of the poorer classes. To the last he was as forward in promoting Evangelical preaching as he was sternly opposed to Romanism and Ritualism. But, although he encouraged such efforts as those of Messrs. Moody and Sankey, he did not sympathise with the mode of operations adopted by the Salvation Army in their directly religious work. " Reverence," said he, " must be the basis of all true religion " ; and this quality he considered at that time was sadly lacking among the Salvationists.

It may not be generally known to our readers that up to the year 1855 there was in this land of religious liberty an Act of Parliament in force and in operation which made it illegal for more than twenty persons, above the members of a household, to meet together for reading the Bible and religious worship, unless the place of meeting was licensed, under a penalty of fine and imprisonment. So recently as 1820, Lord Barham, afterwards Lord Gainsborough, was fined £40—£20 for each meeting—for holding religious meetings in his house when he was unwell and unable to use the village schoolroom. In 1854 a magistrate in a northern county, finding great religious destitution in his densely populated neighbourhood, instituted religious meetings in a large cottage on his estate. He was threatened with proceedings for a breach of the Conventicle Act, and, being a magistrate, did not dare to set the law at defiance, and the meetings were given up. " The gentleman in question," said Lord Shaftesbury, " might have had a cock-fight, jumping in sacks, or any sort of amusement, and nobody could have objected to it ; but the moment this gentleman, commiserating the religious destitution of the people, went to their cottages, read to them a chapter in the Bible, and joined with them in religious worship, the law said, 'Mind what you are doing, for if you are caught at this again you will be fined £20.'"

Lord Shaftesbury saw that here was an engine which, in the hands of the High Church party, might be made destructive to many of the institutions he was fostering. In that very year (1854) the London City Mission alone had held no fewer than 25,318 meetings, of which 22,000 were in direct infringement of the law! In May 1855, therefore, he gave notice of a motion to repeal the obnoxious clauses of the Act which related to this prohibition.

The Bishop of Oxford (Wilberforce) and the Earl of Derby gave vehement and persistent opposition; many bishops sided with them, and what at first had appeared to Lord Shaftesbury to be merely a matter that would, so soon as the anomaly were pointed out, he remedied, gave rise to a long and anxious struggle. Bishop Wilberforce and Earl Derby succeeded in getting the Bill referred to a Select Committee, where it was so terribly mauled and mangled that Lord Shaftesbury moved its rejection in a masterly and memorable speech—in which he trod under foot all the proposed clauses that required for such services the presence of a "licensed" curate, and that prayer, if offered, should only be by the permission of the incumbent or bishop, and so on, and claimed that "every man should have a perfect right to worship God when and how he pleased—to worship in his own house, with his neighbours, in any number, and at any time ; that this should not be a mere privilege, but a right, unless it could be shown that public morality or public safety would be endangered by it."

The effect of this speech, and that of Lord Brougham who followed, was that the Bill of the Earl of Derby was withdrawn, and a little later on Lord Shaftesbury's Religious Worship Bill, enabling every householder to use his house for religious worship free from the fear of pains and penalties, or the interference of any power, judicial or ecclesiastical, passed into law.

Two years later (1857) a series of Special Religious Services were held in Exeter Hall on Sunday evenings, at which some of the "Shaftesbury Bishops," among other ecclesiastics, took an active part. The audiences averaged about 5000 persons, while hundreds were unable to gain admission. But the clergyman of the parish in which Exeter Hall is situated issued an inhibition, and, until the legal point at issue should be settled, the services were suspended. The Nonconformists then stepped in by mutual arrangement, and Lord Shaftesbury brought forward a Religious Worship Act Amendment Bill to make a rector's sanction unnecessary when there were more than 2000 parishioners. This was strenuously opposed by Bishop Wilberforce and his party, and by consent the question was adjourned until the following year, when Archbishop Tait brought in his Bill for Legalising Special Services in connection with the Church of England in unconsecrated buildings. " The Bishops and Lord

Shaftesbury," says the *Record*, "each succeeded in tearing to pieces the Bill of the other, with the result that nothing at all was done."

But a direct outcome of the Exeter Hall services was the inauguration of special evening services in St. Paul's Cathedral and Westminster Abbey, and the holding of Sunday evening services in the metropolitan theatres. The latter movement may be said to have been "founded" by Lord Shaftesbury, in so far as any movement that could not possibly be inaugurated or sustained except by the united efforts of many, may be ascribed to the labours of an individual. Seven London theatres were opened for religious services in the first two months of 1860, with an average attendance of over 20,000 persons. At these services Lord Shaftesbury frequently "assisted" by reading the Scriptures, giving out the hymns, or briefly explaining the aim in view. His standpoint was this :—

"To aid the progress of the general improvement is the object of these special services. No one contemplates them as a permanent system ; our desire is to fell the trees, to clear the jungle, to remove impediments. We hope to bring thousands of our ignorant and neglected brethren to think about Christianity. Having learned it, they will, we trust, pursue it ; and, rising above their attendance at the theatre, attach themselves to the Church of England, or some one or other of the recognised and established forms of worship."

Of course the feelings of the "unco' guid" were violated ; and on February 24th, 1860, Lord Dungannon called attention in the House of Lords to the performance of Divine service at Sadler's Wells and other theatres by clergymen of the Church of England on Sunday evenings, and moved a resolution "that such services being highly irregular and inconsistent with order, are calculated to injure rather than advance the progress of sound religious principles in the metropolis and throughout the country."

In one of the best speeches he ever delivered Lord Shaftesbury replied to this charge, and for two or three hours kept the "statue gallery" of the peers spellbound as he told the story of the movement, the inability of the churches to cope with the irreligion of the masses, and the proved good that these services had accomplished. He flatly denied, from personal experience, the charges of Lord Dungannon, that the meetings were in any way disorderly, and he concluded with this forcible appeal, which is worthy of repetition to-day :—

"My lords, you must perceive the rising struggle to preach the Gospel among this mighty mass of human beings. Can you be indifferent to it ? I ask whether you are prepared, as members of the Church of England, to see the Church stand aloof and the whole of this movement given up exclusively to the Dissenters ? Will you say to those destitute and hungering men, ' We can give you no sort of food. Come, if you like, to Episcopal churches and chapels, and there you shall be preached to in stiff, steady, buckram style. We will have you within walls consecrated in due and official form ; otherwise you shall never hear, from us at least, one word of Gospel truth'? Are you prepared to admit that the Church of England, despite the pressing and fearful necessity, is bound so tightly by rule and rubric, and law and custom, that she can do none of the work? . . . In that case the people who are benefited by these services will reply, 'Let the Nonconformists, then, do the work, but let the Church of England take up her real position as the Church of a sect, and not that of a nation ; she has been applied to and found wanting, and let us follow those who have called us to the knowledge of the truth.' "

Lord Dungannon withdrew his motion.

It would be foreign to our present purpose to enter at length into the purely ecclesiastical questions in which Lord Shaftesbury for so many years stood forward as the champion of the Low Church party, but our work would be very incomplete if it did not allude to his unprecedented position as " Bishop-maker "—to use the designation given to him by Bishop Wilberforce.

Lord Shaftesbury was a sincere admirer of Lord Palmerston. This admiration was partly due to family reasons. Lady Shaftesbury's mother, after the death (in 1837) of her first husband, Earl Cowper, married Lord Palmerston in 1839, and became famous as the hostess of a brilliant *salon*. This relationship

brought Lord Palmerston into close intimacy with
Lord Shaftesbury, and, opposite as the two men
were in almost every respect, each highly esteemed
the intrinsic worth of the other, and a warm friendship
sprang up between them.

During Lord Palmerston's administrations the
amount and variety of Church patronage that fell
to his bestowal was unprecedented in history. It
consisted of "twenty-five mitres and ten deaneries;
including three appointments to English and two to
Irish archbishoprics, sixteen English and four Irish
bishoprics, and ten English deaneries." According to
Lord Shaftesbury himself, Lord Palmerston did "not
know, in theology, Moses from Sydney Smith," and
that being the case it was perfectly natural that
he should turn to the man he implicitly trusted,
and who had his entire confidence, in making these
appointments. It is a mistake, however, to suppose
that *every* appointment was made at the suggestion
of Lord Shaftesbury, and equally a mistake to suppose that the appointments were given exclusively,
or even approximately so, to Evangelicals.

The principle on which Lord Shaftesbury acted in
his recommendations was this:—

"He (Palmerston), at once, and from the very first,
gave me his confidence on these matters, and I very
early determined to look at every vacancy, not from
my own, but from his point of view. Many fit men
passed before me whom I would, had *I* been Prime
Minister, have raised to high places in the Church,

and so I told him ; 'but,' I added, 'I do not advise you to do so, because you could not maintain them, if questioned, on the same grounds as myself, nor allege the same reasons. I must consider your position, the difficulties you have to contend against, the legitimate objections, even in such matters, that beset the path of a public man, and one, from his special office and responsibility, by no means in the attitude and powers of a private patron. I must propose what you and I can defend, not that which could be defended by myself alone.'" *

The principle on which Lord Palmerston acted in making the appointments was this :—

" I have never considered ecclesiastical appointments as patronage to be given away for grace and favour, and for personal or political objects. The choice to be made of persons to fill dignities in the Church must have a great influence on many important matters ; and I have always endeavoured, in making such appointments, to choose the best man I could find, without any regard to the wishes of those who may have recommended candidates for choice." †

We must now pass on to the survey of some of those social philanthropies and reforms in which Lord Shaftesbury was a prime mover, and which have not yet been touched upon in these pages.

---

* "Life and Work," etc., vol. iii., p. 196.
† Lord Palmerston to Lord Carlisle. Quoted in " Life and Work," etc., p. 192.

He was, as it would be considered in these days, a somewhat strict Sabbatarian, and every encroachment on the sanctity of the seventh day he stoutly resisted. He objected to Sunday labour in the Post Office, and in 1850 made himself the most unpopular and roundly-abused man in the kingdom, by obtaining the stoppage of Sunday postal deliveries throughout the country for the space of three weeks, when an inquiry having been moved for, the resolution he had carried, and the order of the Postmaster-General under it, were rescinded. He succeeded in passing a "Sunday Closing of Public Houses Act" in 1854, but it was repealed in the following year. He was the sworn foe of every agitation for opening museums and places of entertainment of any kind on Sunday, and protested strongly against the playing of bands in the metropolitan parks on that day. Holding these views, it was only consistent that he should identify himself with the Lord's Day Observance Society,¹ the Working Men's Lord's Day Rest Association, and other kindred organisations.

"Your political liberties," he said to the members of the Working Men's Lord's Day Rest Association, "are more secure under the charter of the Sabbath than they can be under all the charters which were ever given by any of our kings, including that of Runnymede itself. That charter is greater than any other that God has ever given to man. It is as great as the sanctity of His own Book."

Severe as his views may be considered on the

Sunday question, they were broadly charitable on the question of holidays and relaxation of toil for the people. When Lord Dunraven brought forward his famous resolution in 1883, in favour of the Sunday Opening of the National Museums and Picture Galleries, Lord Shaftesbury met it by moving an amendment, "That such institutions as the British Museum and the National Gallery should be opened on weekday evenings to the public between the hours of seven and ten in the evening, at least three days in the week," an amendment that was carried without a division.

He took up a position of characteristic consistency by standing at the head of the Early Closing Movement from its commencement in 1842. "In what way," he would ask, "can you improve the observance of the Sabbath so effectually as by giving a time for amusement and repose on every Saturday afternoon? And I maintain that all those who have concurred with me in opposition to the motion for opening places of amusement on the Lord's Day are bound to go along with those who entertain the opinion that I do—that if we refuse to give them that form of recreation on the Lord's Day, we are bound to do what we can to give them some form of recreation on some other day."

In the rise and progress of the Young Men's Christian Association he was deeply interested, and from its commencement in 1844 to the end of his life he remained its president. "I have always looked upon this Association," he said, "and all kindred

Associations in all parts of the United Kingdom and in America, as grand cities of refuge from the commercial life, individually and collectively, of the several nations—places where young men, coming from a distance, and removed from all parental influence and all the influence of domestic life, may find shelter, and where they may learn the way of salvation, and obtain courage and confidence to walk in it." Nor was he indifferent to that other side of the work of the Association which tends to the salvation of the body. "When people say we should think more of the soul and less of the body," he said on one occasion, "my answer is that the same God who made the soul made the body also. It is an inferior work, perhaps, but nevertheless it is His work, and it must be treated and cared for according to the end for which it was formed—fitness for His service." When the Association added to its prayer-meetings and Bible-classes a gymnasium and athletic training classes, the welcome innovation met with Lord Shaftesbury's marked approval. Thus, when referring to the gymnasium, he said: "When I see the vast number of young men before me who are engaged the whole day long in heated rooms, some never sitting down, some never standing up, occupied in businesses which are not conducive to physical health, I feel that it is absolutely necessary that the body should be regarded ; that you should be able to develop your muscular and physical faculties and get them into order and shape ; and that the body should be cherished in an honourable, noble, and becoming way, and made more adapted and suitable to the great intellectual purposes of which it is only the depository. I hope you will use the gymnasium well."

In like manner he delighted to forward by every means in his power the splendid work of the Ragged School Union and other societies in their beneficent schemes for sending poor children from the crowded courts and alleys of the great city for "a day in the country," and in aiding every movement for providing playgrounds and open spaces.

The absorbing interest taken by Lord Shaftesbury in Ragged School work brought him into strange company, and none stranger, perhaps, than the costermongers of London, whose families furnished the largest portion of the Ragged scholars. Johnson's definition of a costermonger, it seems, as "a person who sells apples," is pronounced "gammon" by the fraternity, one of whom is said to have substituted the following for it: "A cove wot works werry 'ard for a werry poor livin', and is always a-bein' hinterfered with, and blowed up, and moved hon and fined, and sent to quod by the beaks and bobbies." Among this curious tribe—who herd together by thousands in the neighbourhood of Golden Lane, which is bounded by Goswell Street, Old Street, Bunhill Row, and Chiswell Street—Mr. W. J. Orsman, civil servant, evangelist, and, later, member of the London County Council and the London School Board, organised a mission, still in existence and doing as noble and useful a work as any organisation for the benefit of

the poor in London ; and when Lord Shaftesbury
heard of it he at once offered his services and became
its president.   He won his way to the hearts of the
costers in a surprising manner, and was soon as much
' at home " with them in their sphere as he was in his
own mansion in Grosvenor Square.   He fought their
battles, attended their meetings, and brought influence
to bear on their condition through vestries and parish
magistrates.   Of the "Barrow and Donkey Club,"
which had been instituted, he enrolled himself a
member, and subscribed for a barrow of his own,
which bore his arms and motto, and was lent out to
deserving young members who had not yet attained
to the honours of proprietorship.   It was his delight
to call himself a "coster" and spend a social evening
with the "brethren."   He told them that if at any
time they had any grievance they wanted redressed
they should write to him, and being asked his address,
he assured them that any letter sent to Grosvenor
Square, with "K.G. and Coster" after his name, would
be sure to find him !

In the institution of donkey shows and prizes, much
good was done in rescuing many hundreds of poor
beasts from a life of ill-treatment to one of comparative happiness, and in this department of the work
Lord Shaftesbury was always ready to lend his assistance by distributing prizes and speaking on the
economy of kindness.   On one occasion (1875), the
costers invited their president to meet them to receive
a presentation.   To his surprise he found over a
thousand of the fraternity assembled, with many friends

of all classes; and presently, after taking his seat, a fine donkey, decorated with ribbons, was introduced, led up on to the platform, and solemnly presented to the earl. Lord Shaftesbury, having vacated the chair in the donkey's favour, stood with his arm round its neck while he briefly returned thanks, adding, with a touch of pathos, "When I have passed away from this life I desire to have no more said of me than that I have done my duty, as the poor donkey has done his, with patience and unmurmuring resignation." On the retirement of the donkey from the platform, his lordship begged the reporters to state that "the donkey having vacated the chair, the place was taken by Lord Shaftesbury!"

His interest in costers, and street dealers generally, brought him into contact with the "Watercress and Flower Girls' Mission," and soon after the death of his wife he established a fund in her memory, the "Emily Loan Fund," to assist deserving flower and watercress girls in times of necessity, and especially in the winter months, when the sources of their incomes failed. "Thus, one poor woman would make application for the loan of a baked-potato oven, a coffee stall, a barrow and a board for the sale of whelks, or any other article by which she might see a reasonable prospect of earning a living." The system on which loans were granted was simple and safe, and the institution has done in the past, and is still doing, incalculable good to a hard-working and industrious class.

Always a lover of dumb animals, and especially of

dogs, Lord Shaftesbury rendered important aid in 1876 in founding the Society for the Protection of Animals from Vivisection—"a diabolical system," he said, "the thought of which distresses me night and day." On two occasions he spoke at length in the House of Lords in support of Bills for its total abolition. His argument was that, whether vivisection was conducive to the advancement of science or the reverse, there was one great preliminary consideration—"on what authority did his opponents rest their right to subject God's creatures to unspeakable sufferings? The animals were His creatures, as we are His creatures, and 'His tender mercies,' we are told in the Bible, 'are over *all* His works.'" Whatever view may be taken of this much-debated subject, it is interesting to know that Lord Shaftesbury never altered his opinion on it, and from the establishment of the Society to the close of his life he practically directed all its public action.

Brought into contact as he was throughout his life with so much of sin and its consequences and of moral evil generally, he was deeply interested in every effort that was made to provide pure literature for the people. Generations of magistrates had declared that immoral literature was the cause of an enormous percentage of youthful crime. Before the passing of Lord Campbell's Act the traffic in obscene literature went on practically unchecked, and this "death fountain" sent forth its impure waters freely to corrupt and poison the youth of the nation. The importation from France was extremely large, the very titles of pictures and translated pamphlets being unfit to mention; and, besides the supplies coming from foreign sources, "the printed abomination which went forth from Holywell Street in a single week was reckoned to be sufficient to corrupt the morals of the entire youth of London." But this was an open and seen danger. What he dreaded, and what he foresaw advancing as a rapid tide and spreading everywhere, was sensational literature so fascinating in itself that the evil in it was not readily perceived, compositions "the most insidious, the most attractive, the most skilful, and the most deceptive of all the literature that ever emanated from the minds of men."

"I was led to look into works like those to which I allude very seriously," he said in one of his public speeches, "and I was struck by the beauty of the composition and by the artful way in which the most wicked and foul ideas were conveyed. I observed, particularly, the manner in which they were especially addressed to the minds of young men and young women; how the most pure-minded young man, or the most modest young woman, might read one of those works twice or thrice without discerning the object of the composition, and perhaps would never discern it until the poison had entered the soul. In fact, these things had been written with so much care, that I would defy any writer that ever was, or any writer that ever will be, to draw an Act of Parliament containing clauses that would suffice to put down such literature as that."

The Society for Promoting Christian Knowledge, the Religious Tract Society, the Pure Literature Society, and other societies of a kindred nature, found in Lord Shaftesbury a willing and an able supporter.

Although we have confined ourselves to a record of Lord Shaftesbury's labours on behalf of the poor and suffering in his own country, it must not be inferred that he was either indifferent or inactive in relation to the claims of the needy, and the necessity for social reforms, in other lands. He brought before Parliament in 1844 the case of the Ameers of Scinde, who were suffering imprisonment and deprivation of their rights from no fault, as he conceived, of their own; he took up the cause of persecuted Jews in Russia and elsewhere; of Pomare, the Queen of Tahiti, a convert to Christianity; for forty years he waged war against the opium trade, "fraught with misery and ruin to tens of thousands of the Chinese people"; it was he who organised the Sanitary Commission to the Crimea—"that Commission," said Miss Florence Nightingale, "saved the British Army"; he stood forth as the champion of the women and children of India who were suffering under grinding oppression in the Bombay factories, under a system as barbarous as that which once existed in this country, and aggravated by the heat of the climate and the disregard of a weekly day of rest; it was he who, in 1861, after a famine had desolated a large part of India, moved an Address to the Crown praying Her Majesty to take into her immediate and serious consideration the means of extending throughout India, as widely as possible, the best system of irrigation and internal navigation, and thus became the "first man in Parliament to apprehend and demonstrate that the wealth of India depended upon its waters, that its wealth was wasted by neglecting them, and that it might be indefinitely augmented by utilising them. He was, moreover, the pioneer of that policy, long since adopted, of not depending only on one source of cotton supply."

When Lord Ashley was a young man of twenty-seven he wrote in his diary :—

"*August 3rd*, 1828. . . . Am happy to have had the means of spending £5 in a good cause—nothing less than a subscription to a fund which may educate a young girl, and save her, perhaps, from misery and prostitution. Taste and inborn vice will take enough to that career without the number being swollen by the victims of treachery and distress. I shall give any money that may be wanted."

Nearly sixty years later that same subject lay very near to his heart, and occupied much of the time of his last working days. On July 30th, 1880, he supported "a strong Bill, almost a fearful Bill, and capable no doubt of enormous abuse," to prohibit little girls under fourteen from living in houses of ill-fame. A year later he took up the case of girls ensnared into foreign lands, and Brussels especially, for immoral purposes. In 1883 he supported a Bill in the House of Lords for the protection of young girls ; later in the same year he was defeated upon an amendment to protect helpless women and defenceless girls from insults and dangers in the streets, and in 1884 he spoke at the Mansion House in aid of a new society for protection of children against cruelty.

———————

On October 1st, 1885, Lord Shaftesbury ceased from his labours and entered into rest. His name stands out pre-eminently, and will live for ever, as *the* Social Reformer of the Victorian era.

We have given elsewhere the full story of his public, domestic, and inner life, and our estimate of his character and work. We therefore conclude this survey of his career as philanthropist and social reformer in the words of another :—

"His heart was green and vigorous to the last. No chills of age could lessen the passionate warmth of his pity for the poor and suffering ; no invading feebleness of voice or limb hold him back from advocating the cause of the defenceless and oppressed. For these his zeal burnt with an unquenchable fire ; for these he toiled as long as the faculty to do anything remained to him ; for these he could have wished still to live and labour, even when the infirmities of fourscore-and-four years had made life a burden. ' I cannot bear,' he said in his last days, ' to leave the world with all the misery in it.' It is this unreserved, this absolute sacrifice of himself, body and soul, to the work of alleviating that misery, which encircles his name with a glory. . . . His career is the national inheritance of the English-speaking race, as an immortal protest against a life of self-seeking, and a noble lesson how worldly rank and station may be redeemed from moral insignificance, and consecrated to the best interests of humanity. 'Love, serve,' was his ancestral motto ; to love and serve was the paramount, abiding law of his existence, till death gently brought him the rest which, living, he would never seek for himself." *

* *Quarterly Review*, No. 327, January 1887.

INDEX.

Printed by Hazell, Watson, & Viney, Ld., London and Aylesbury.

JAMES NISBET & CO.'S
List of New and Forthcoming Works.

Novels and Stories.

THE RIP'S REDEMPTION. A Trooper's Story. By E. LIVINGSTON PRESCOTT, Author of "Scarlet and Steel," "A Mask and a Martyr," etc. With Frontispiece by ENOCH WARD. Extra crown 8vo. Gilt top, 6s.

LADY ROSALIND ; or, Family Feuds. By MRS. MARSHALL, Author of "Only Susan," "The Close of St. Christopher," etc. With Frontispiece by ENOCH WARD. Extra crown 8vo. Gilt top. 6s.

A FIGHT FOR FREEDOM. A Tale of the Land of the Czar. A Book for Boys. By GORDON STABLES, M.D., R.N., Author of "The Pearl Divers," etc. With Illustration by CHAS. WHYMPER. Extra crown 8vo. Gilt edges. 5s.

IN THE SWING OF THE SEA. A Book for Boys. By J. MACDONALD OXLEY, Author of "On the World's Roof," etc. Illustrated by W. B. LANCE. Extra crown 8vo. 3s. 6d.

HALF-HOURS IN EARLY NAVAL ADVENTURE. A New Volume in the "Half-Hour Library." With many Illustrations. Crown 8vo. 2s. 6d. With gilt edges, 3s.

GERALD AND DOLLY. A Story of Two Small People. By D'ESTERRE. Illustrated by W. B. Lance. Crown 8vo. 2s.

THE OLDER BROTHER. By PANSY. With Four Illustrations. Crown 8vo. 2s. 6d.

Theological and Devotional.

THE MINISTRY OF INTERCESSION. A Plea for more Prayer. By the Rev. ANDREW MURRAY, Author of "Abide in Christ." Small crown 8vo. 1s. 6d.

THE LORD'S TABLE : A help to the right observance of the Holy Supper. By the Rev. ANDREW MURRAY. Pott 8vo. 1s.

OLD TESTAMENT SYNONYMS. By CANON GIRDLESTONE Revised and re-written from an earlier work. Demy 8vo. 12s.

PICTURES OF THE EAST. A set of forty full-page original Drawings to illustrate the Life of Our Lord and the Preaching of St. Paul. With Notes and Explanations. By Mrs. RENDEL HARRIS. Imperial 8vo. 8s. 6d.

THE FAITH OF CENTURIES. A series of Essays and Lectures by well-known writers and preachers, re-stating and explaining in a form both scholarly and popular the essential doctrines of the Christian Faith. Edited by the Rev. W. E. BOWEN, and containing contributions, among others, from the Bishop of Rochester, Bishop BARRY, Archdeacon SINCLAIR, Canon SCOTT-HOLLAND, Canon NEWBOLT, Professor RYLE, and the Rev. T. B. STRONG. Extra crown 8vo. 7s. 6d.

SHARPENED TOOLS FOR BUSY WORKERS. A Book of Facts, Figures, Quotations, Illustrations, etc., for Christian Workers. By JOHN S. DOIDGE. Extra crown 8vo. 5s. nett.

THE CHURCH OF CHRIST. By the Rev. E. A. LITTON. Revised and re-written from an earlier work. With an Introduction by the Rev. F. J. CHAVASSE. Extra crown 8vo. 5s.

STRATEGIC POINTS IN THE WORLD'S CONQUEST. The Universities and Colleges as related to the Progress of Christianity. Specially designed for Christian Students. With Map. By JOHN R. MOTT. Crown 8vo. Gilt top. 3s. 6d.

INSPIRED THROUGH SUFFERING. By the Rev. DAVID O. MEARS, D.D. Crown 8vo. 2s. 6d.

WHAT IS SIN? A Volume of Select Sermons preached before the University of Oxford. By Canon MCCORMICK, D.D. Crown 8vo. 2s. 6d.

HOW TO OBTAIN FULNESS OF POWER. By R. A. TORREY, Author of "How to Bring Men to Christ," etc. Crown 8vo. 1s. 6d.

HOW WE LEARNED IT. Talks and Stories on the Lord's Prayer. By Lady COOTE. Small crown 8vo. 1s. 6d.

WHY AM I A CHRISTIAN? By the DEAN OF NORWICH, Author of "The Christian's Start." Crown 8vo. 1s. 6d.

PREACHERS OF TO-DAY. Small crown 8vo. 1s., in paper covers ; 1s. 6d. cloth.

> Sin and its Conquerors ; or, The Conquest of Sin. By DEAN FARRAR.
> The Endless Choice. By the Rev. W. J. DAWSON.
> The Glory of the Lord. By Canon EYTON.
> The New Law. By Archdeacon SINCLAIR.

CONDITIONAL IMMORTALITY. Letters by Sir GEORGE STOKES, Bart. Long fcap 8vo. 1s.

THE PRACTICE OF THE PRESENCE OF GOD. Letters and Conversations of Nicholas Herman of Lorraine (Brother Lawrence). With an Introduction by Mrs. PEARSALL SMITH. Small crown 8vo. 1s.

FIGHT AND WIN. Talks with Lads about the Battle of Life. By the Rev. G. EVERARD, M.A. Pott 8vo. 1s.

New Volumes in the "Deeper Life" Series.

Crown 8vo. 2s. 6d.

THE CHRIST LIFE. By the Rev. J. B. Figgis, M.A., Author of "Christ and Full Salvation," "The Anointing," etc.

CONSECRATED WORK. By the Rev. J. Elder Cumming, D.D.

History, Biography and General Literature.

A CHILD'S HISTORY OF ENGLAND. By Mrs. F. S. Boas. Specially designed for young children by an experienced teacher of History, and revised by the Regius Professor of Modern History in the University of Oxford. Profusely Illustrated. Crown 8vo. 2s.

THE LIFE OF LORD SHAFTESBURY, as Social Reformer. By Edwin Hodder. Crown 8vo. 2s. 6d.

A CENTURY OF MISSIONARY MARTYRS. A Series of Biographical Studies in Missionary Work. By S. F. Harris, Author of "Earnest Young Heroes." With Frontispiece. Crown 8vo. 2s. 6d.

SEVEN YEARS IN SIERRA LEONE. The Story of the Work of William A. B. Johnson, Missionary of the Church Missionary Society from 1816 to 1823, in Regent's Town, Sierra Leone, Africa. By the Rev. A. T. Pierson, D.D., Author of "The New Acts of the Apostles," etc. Crown 8vo. 3s. 6d.

HEALTH IN AFRICA. A Medical Handbook for European Residents and Travellers in Central and Southern Africa. By Dr. David Kerr Cross, Medical Officer to the British Central Africa Protectorate. With an Introduction by Sir H. H. Johnston, K.C.B. Profusely illustrated with diagrams and plans. Crown 8vo. 3s. 6d.

MADE EXCEEDING GLAD. A Memoir of W. J. Neethling. By Mrs. Neethling. With an Introduction by the Rev. A. Murray. Royal 16mo. 6d.

A complete list, post free, on application to the publishers.

JAMES NISBET & CO., LIMITED,
21, Berners Street, W.

Printed in Great Britain
by Amazon